STRANGERS' FOREST

*By the same author*

THE DEVIL OF ASKE
THE MALVIE INHERITANCE
WHITTON'S FOLLY
NORAH
THE GREEN SALAMANDER

# Strangers' Forest

PAMELA HILL

ST. MARTIN'S PRESS   NEW YORK

**Library of Congress Cataloging in Publication Data**

Hill, Pamela.
  Strangers' forest.

  I. Title.
PZ4.H648St  1978  [PR6058.I446]  823'.9'14
ISBN 0-312-76426-X          77-9183

78000618

AUTHOR'S NOTE

On enquiry, I find that child marriages took place in this country until 1816. The date of this story is set about thirty-five years earlier.                                             P.H.

## One

It must have been early September when I, Primrose Tebb, climbed into the apple tree, because the crabs were just ripe, and further off, where the ground began to slope towards the marsh, the different greens of elm and ash and willow were dulled. I have always noticed colours and like to try and paint them, paying as much heed to that as other young women do to their clothes. That day mine were not notable. I was wearing my cousin Thornton's old torn shirt and breeches which he had long outgrown, because I felt comfortable in them and they made climbing easier. This however was not a climb of any difficulty, because I did not even have to start from the ground. Beyond my bedroom window-sill, to be reached if one stretched far enough, lay a thick branch to be crawled along, then there was a secret place like a hollow where long ago a limb had broken off in a storm. The bark made a little puffed scar round the broken place. I often sat there in summer, for no one knew where I was when the leaves were thick. Now, however, there was some risk. The crabs hung within reach and presently I would pick them and stuff them one after the other into the bosom of my shirt, though truth to tell they were sour

and not good eating, or worth all the trouble. But to do something without either being observed or admonished gave me
pleasure, as my aunt was trying to bring me up to behave as a
lady and I did not feel that I could contrive it. She would not
have approved of my wearing her only son's breeches and I had
had to purloin them when nobody was looking. If I kept out of
the way, there would be no trouble.

It has occurred to me since then that we all, every single
one of us at Pless, had our own lives that were kept separate
from aunt Milhall's, and perhaps she had hers that she kept
from us. Nevertheless I could tell what everyone in the house
might be doing at this moment, intent on their own concerns:
my father, seated by the hall fire as always after noon, would
be turning his ruined mind and trembling hands to chess,
which he played against himself as there were no neighbours
except the Admiral, who did not visit. So the assembled kings
and queens and rooks and pawns hardly changed on father's
table as week followed week, so intent was he on the one thing
that he could still do adequately. Aunt Milhall would be
fussing over jams and pickles in the store-room. Thornton,
now he had helped my father into the hall, would be idling,
or cleaning his gun which he did not do often enough, or talking
about going to shoot tern on the marsh, or going to the tavern
or wherever else he pleased. I have never known anyone who
pleased himself so much as Thornton. Penuel, his sister, would
be pressing ferns into an album she kept, her fair head bent
and her mouth pressed close like a nun's. Since she had become
a widow Penuel spent half the year with us and the other half
at her house in town, and when she was at Pless she was always
out on the moors and marshes and in the lanes collecting plants,
as though she cared for nothing else. I believe this to have
been true, for on the rare occasions when there was company at
our house she kept her eyes to the ground and did not answer
unless spoken to. My aunt had forced her into marriage while
young and the bridegroom had been an old judge who groped

after Penuel's beauty. When he died—the marriage lasted about four years—he left Penuel with enough money to live on and keep a town house, provided she did not marry again. But it was plain she had no wish to.

So there we all were, with our different ways of passing the time. But what I saw from the apple-tree that afternoon was to change all of that, all our lives, mine especially. How could I have foreseen it then? I was only twelve years old, and had never been out in the world or indeed very often beyond Pless garden.

This is how it happened. I had gathered my crabs and had set my teeth into a promising one, but it was so sour I threw it from me, hard into the distance, and then I heard a cry. It was not helpless, like a child or an animal in pain, but deep and startled, almost angry; a man's shout. I took one look between the leaves and saw what had happened and faster than I had come along it I wriggled back along my weight-bearing branch to the shelter of my room. For moments I hid against the wall, pressing my hand to where the apples lay in my bosom, then Thornton's shirt, which was threadbare, burst and they rolled on to the floor and I began to laugh. Then I stopped laughing as the voices of two men came nearer.

I turned round, and looked out of the window, standing at the side where one cannot be seen. Beyond the screen of leaves I saw them come; a white man and a dark. They had stopped troubling themselves about who had thrown the apple, which must have hit one or other of them, and had returned to their business. What that might be made me very curious indeed. I stayed close by my window, to see and not be seen. This is easy if one knows how.

I took note of the men. One was of middle height and sandy-haired, the kind of man who might be met with every day. I did not think about his age; I have since learned that at that time he was twenty-four. This would have seemed to me a great age. However I did not stop to look at Andrew Farquharson further as I was more interested in his companion, who now that I could see him more clearly was not black but the colour of copper. He was the first coloured man I had ever seen. He was tall, with blue-black hair hanging straight to the shoulder without a riband to tie it back, and his skin shone and he had a great thrusting nose like a hawk's beak and small jetty eyes. His clothes were ordinary, and shabby; the cloth coat strained across his powerful shoulders, and he seemed like a lithe animal who could have stripped and been happier naked. For a moment he stared across to where I had been in the tree and I had the feeling that although nobody else had known I had been there, he knew. I withdrew further into the room.

I could not make out what it was the two men were doing in our orchard. They had a stick and were poking at the ground, and from time to time would bend down and scoop up the mossy earth in little handfuls, and examine it. For a moment I felt like running downstairs to tell everyone there were two strange men in the grounds and then I thought better of it; in the first place I would be scolded for wearing Thornton's breeches, and in the second it was unlikely aunt Milhall did not know they were there. Everything that happened at Pless had to be approved and known by my aunt Milhall, because my father could no longer look after his own concerns. She had come to us when my mother was dying and had stayed ever since. This being the case, I remained where I was. If the two men meant any harm, which was unlikely, Thornton's stupid dog, or Thornton's gun, or even our old servant Bethia who feared nothing and nobody and had been with us since my mother came as a bride, would deal with them. In fact so few strangers ever came to Pless that the two men might be rather a diversion than a nuisance. But I could not rid myself of a feeling of anger that they had scooped up the earth of our orchard. When all is said, it was our earth.

They had moved closer and now I could hear what they were saying. The sandy-haired man spoke in the uncompromising way of the Scots and the other spoke broken English. I could hear the Scot say pleasantly, in a way which told me that he had forgotten about being hit with the apple, "This is the place, Saginaw. We could have searched for years had it not been for that good fellow Arnison."

This intrigued me very much and told me that at any rate the men were not trespassing. Arnison was our lawyer, who rode over twice a year to dine, and having gone over the books with aunt Milhall always rode away again with a longer face than even he ordinarily possessed. Then another thing began to trouble me; were these men going to rent the orchard and do some harm to it? I loved our orchard at Pless. It had every imaginable tree and shrub growing in the wildest profusion, with jew's-mallow gripping everything: for once there had been a Tebb squire who had gone to London to make himself known in high-born circles, and had seen the gardens the Dutch king was busy planting at Hampton Court. The squire had then come home with ideas which were too big for his purse, which was already depleted, and had planted the estate, so that we were still short-changed by reason of that and also my father's gaming-debts in his wild youth. No one tended the rare shrubs now, but I loved every one. One could wander for an hour dragged at by thistles and cleavers, and pick strange leaves and blossoms to put in a jug in one's room or simply look at them where they grew. The orchard stretched for almost two acres and then beyond on one side there was the marshland and on the other the moor. All of it would be mine, I knew, when father died, but I felt as if it were so already. I loved Pless, and he had never done so. Best of all I loved the little stream which dried up sometimes in summer, but which at other seasons of the year would have water-crowfoot and wild iris and great clumps of yellow marsh-marigold, and in spring the primroses studded all the further bank like pale stars. Often my poor mother had sat there and stared at them and had thought that if when I were born I were to be a girl, she would call me after the flowers, which consoled her a little for the disappointment of her marriage. Bethia had told me all that. I could scarcely remember mother for myself, for she had died when I was four. I can recall that she had kind eyes and a pock-marked face, and was never angry with me.

Now these two strange men said the orchard was the place they had been looking for. I felt like hitting out at them with another apple. But no doubt I would learn more by using my eyes and ears and keeping silence, I had already grown used to doing all of these things.

There was a scratching at the door and I knew that it could not be aunt Milhall, who always marched straight in. It must be Penuel. I turned from where I was arranging the apples in a row on top of my clothes-chest, and ran to lift the latch. Penuel was standing there as I had hoped, looking as she always did, which is to say as beautiful as an enchanted princess, locked up in an ivory tower. I am not fanciful when I say that regarding her tower, Penuel herself held the key. She was at that time twenty-two years old. She had a slender shape and long slender hands and feet, and her hair was straight as falling rain and the silvery-gold colour of ripe barley. It was caught in a knot at the nape of her neck. Her eyes were not blue, as might have been expected, but instead a colour between green and grey, fringed with long lashes darker than her hair. I can just remember, when I was a small child, Penuel as she was when she was young, before her marriage. In those days she had a shining joyous quality, so that she and Thornton, who is floridly handsome, walked side by side like a young god and goddess. But now that was gone. Penuel was like the gown she wore, sober with a high collar, like a schoolmistress. She seldom smiled, although she did so now at sight of me in the breeches. We had always loved one another and when she was with me, and at no time else, Penuel threw off her shyness and prudish ways, as her brother Thornton called them; Thornton would never understand, though I did, what that marriage to an old lecher had done to her. I could hear his taunting voice now, made to some one of our rare visitors. "My sister's naught but a damned nun nowadays, poring over her plants. Never waste your sighs." For many a man, both young and old, would have wasted more than sighs on Penuel, even knowing as they soon did that she would lose her money on remarriage. Whether everyone thought she still mourned her old judge, I cannot tell. I think she wore her mourning about her like a cloak, to shut away love and lovers. When she was at Pless she came and went as she would, out gathering her plants, sometimes not even appearing for dinner.

She was speaking of dinner now. "We are to have guests," she murmured, "and Mama says that I am to help you into the green brocade gown."

"Heavens, why?"

Penuel looked across at the row of apples on the chest and laughed a little. "You have been climbing the tree again," she said.

"It is easy." I knew that she would not tell aunt Milhall where I had been. Instead, she placed herself firmly on my side in the matter.

"When I was little and we would come for holidays to Pless before my father died"—uncle Milhall had survived marriage only a bare ten years, and my aunt wore a lock of his hair, which was fair like Penuel's, in the back of a brooch she affected which had a gilded frame and an agate on the front— "I used to climb the tree sometimes. But I never dared wear breeches as you do. You look like a boy, Primrose. I believe you wish you had been one."

"If I had, father would not have been disappointed in me, and might have mended his ways."

"For pity's sake, child, the things you say!"

"Bethia told me of it. He had wagered his last ten guineas to the Admiral that I should be a son, and then when I was born he had to go out and get drunk on borrowings."

"Sweetheart, you have mud on your cheek. We must wash it off before you go downstairs."

"You have not yet told me why I must wear the green gown."

"Did I have leisure to? You chatter like a bird." Penuel folded her lips cautiously, then opened them again so that I could just see the pearly gleam of small white teeth. "I know that I can trust you, nevertheless," she said, "and so I will tell you what little I know. As I said, we have company; and it is important that you go down and make a good showing, and eat prettily and do not grow pert. It is all of it to do with money about the land, and you know well how badly it is needed." I knew well, also, that Penuel herself was unable to spend her own money in the ways she would have liked, for the judge had tied it all up in trusts and doled-out annuities. I have said that I had learned to listen, and one day when nobody knew I was there I had heard Arnison speak of the matter from where I crouched under the downstairs table, playing with straws.

Now I noted that Penuel had spoken of guests, not of a guest; that meant that the copper man would eat with us and not with Bethia in the kitchen.

"Where have they come from, the two men?" I asked, and then realised that I had let slip my secret and at once, to save time, told Penuel how I had spied them from the tree and hit one with an apple. This made her laugh and she said "Dear me, I hope it is not the one you are to marry."

"I am to *what*?" I was stunned; in her turn Penuel looked confused, and said "Do not betray that I have told you; you were to hear of it later, but I thought it right in any case that you should know, and then you will see how important it is to behave yourself, so that he is pleased with you."

"Which am I to marry, the white man or the brown?" I felt the onset of giggles; this could not be happening to me, Primrose Tebb, aged twelve; no young lady married, as a rule, till she was fifteen, and had had some schooling. It was true that few girls were asked if they liked their bridegrooms, as I knew well enough from Penuel's sad affair. But of the two men, I rather hoped for a copper suitor. It would be more unusual, and our children would be coffee-coloured.

Penuel had looked troubled since I told her of the thrown apple, and said now, with a crease in her white forehead, "I hope that they did not catch sight of you in the tree, or think you a hoyden. Do not speak of it, I pray, at dinner." She thought for a moment and then, my last speech having made itself manifest, said in horror "But of course it is the white man, Primrose! He is a Mr. Andrew Farquharson, and they say he has a great deal of money. Who the other may be I know not, but no doubt he came with Mr. Farquharson from Canada, with their bales of furs."

"Did Mr. Farquharson make his money out of the furs?"

"How do I know, child? I did not ask him. At all events, we must all of us be proud of you tonight; so let me lace the gown on, and comb your hair. It is as tangled as a dog's, and there are leaves in it."

I kept on chattering while Penuel tidied me. "Farquharson is a Scots name, is it not?" I said, remembering the sandy-haired man's accent. I wanted to impress on Penuel the fact that I knew which was which. Pless is in the north of England near the Border and since Penuel had married her judge, she had many Scots acquaintances and her house in Edinburgh was a meeting-place for persons of letters when she entertained. Yes, Penuel said, Farquharson was the same name as Ferguson, only spelt differently, and I spelled the two names out to myself and decided that I might as well become Mrs Farquharson as anything else. The dazzling fact of an offer having been made for me had turned my head a little, for I had always been brought up with the knowledge that I would have no dowry and, in any case, young men in these parts were scarce.

"How did he know I was here?" I asked presently, when

Penuel had got me into a clean petticoat and stays. The stays were hardly worth wearing as my body was still flat, like a child's or a boy's; but aunt Milhall said stay-bones made one stand and sit correctly from the first. Penuel shook her head. "He did not know of you at the start, Primrose," she said. "It was the land that interested him. He is looking for a place to plant some trees. Mr. Arnison the lawyer recommended that he try here, and he has been already twice—you do not know everything, you see—and has had tests made of some kind, so he is very well satisfied. He offered to buy the land, but it is entailed and not for sale, and so it was decided—Mr. Arnison and Mama thought of it, I believe—that if he were to marry you, he could have the use of the land while you are growing up, and would make a settlement on you, which pleases everyone."

It did not please me particularly that I was being married on account of some few acres of marsh, and I said so. Mr. Farquharson might, I felt, have taken a look at me sooner; how did he know that I did not squint or have bad breath? Perhaps he was so much taken up with his trees that it did not matter what I looked like. I put my tongue out at my own reflection in the spotted mirror. Penuel did not see me, for she was removing the crab-apples from the clothes-chest and presently opened it and found the green brocade gown, which had belonged to my mother. It was brocade of Venice. It had been made down, but was still too big for me about the waist and bodice because aunt Milhall had said that they must leave room for my growth. There was a short lace ruff which ought to have fitted about the neck and left bare flesh beneath, but moths had eaten at it and I did not wear it. I stared at myself while Penuel combed my hair. I saw a small dab-featured being with brown curls and white teeth, the left eye-tooth being somewhat crooked. My eyes are dark with long lashes, like mother's. When Penuel had turned away to clean the comb I took two of the apples and stuck them down my dress to make a bosom.

Then I puffed out my cheeks and when Penuel looked at me again she burst out laughing. "Now I am Mrs. Farquharson," I said.

I was proud of my apple-bosom and made Penuel promise to let me keep it until it was time to go down. "Mama will blame me if you appear like that, so be sure to take them out," she said. She left me to go and tidy herself and I paraded and strutted about like a guinea-fowl in my brocaded skirts and wondered about Mr. Farquharson and also about his copper-coloured friend. At least I should see the latter again when we all assembled downstairs for dinner. Then it occurred to me that I might take a peek earlier than that, for my father and Thornton would surely drink wine with the guests before the meal, and aunt Milhall, whose managing nature would never let her absent herself from anything, even men's matters, would be there also. If I placed myself behind one of the great carved balusters which fronted the gallery leading to the stairs, I could see without being seen, and perhaps find out more of what was after all as much my business as anyone's.

I stationed myself, but all I could see as yet was my father, seated by the fire, head jerking helplessly as it sometimes did when his disease changed course. I have heard Bethia say that when he was a young man father had fine looks and finer manners, and that must have been true, for they let him marry my mother on the strength of the tales he told about himself. But by now he was no more than a hulk of bone-white flesh, caring for nothing except his chessmen and his wine. He and I were nothing to one another, and had never been.

My cousin Thornton lounged nearby, helping himself to covert sips of the wine before anyone else came in. I could have called out, but remembered that I was watching in secret; how it showed one things about people! I knew already that Thornton was bone-idle, spoilt, dishonest and treacherous, but none of it was any surprise to me although aunt Milhall doted on him. There had once been a suggestion that he and I should marry, but as no money was to be found on either side it had been considered best that Thornton find himself a rich wife if any offered. I did not care, as apart from the use of his breeches I had little time for Thornton now; as a boy he had been pleasanter.

The visitors entered, and I saw them again by the light of candles. These flared pleasantly on Mr. Farquharson's neat sandy hair, turning it to gold. Otherwise, his face was plain and sensible; I was to discover at table that his skin was freckled. The copper man followed him, keeping in his shadow. He might have been a bodyguard.

The Scotsman apologised for his coat. It was the same he had worn in the orchard. "We did not anticipate the good fortune of being bidden to dinner, sir." It was at this point that I noticed his linen; it was white and clean.

Aunt Milhall's voice came, on her flirtatious note which she used when things were going well. "The occasion, Mr. Farquharson! Did you think we would send you away with never a glimpse of your bride? Fie, sir!"

Thornton poured the wine, and my aunt swept into view. She was a stocky woman with the handsome looks my father may have had before he ruined them. She wore her best bombazine and a goffered widow's cap trembling with jet. Otherwise, we were in no great array apart from my Venice brocade. Father had been put in his old velvet coat as he always was at this hour, and Thornton had not troubled to dress grandly, or even wear hair-powder. He was looking down his nose at the guests and I was uncertain whether his scorn confined itself to the copper man or included Mr. Farquharson, whose airs were more homespun than ours. I wondered again how he had grown rich.

Then Penuel came downstairs, wearing a lilac gown which became her. I saw Mr. Farquharson's eyes light on her, and it was at this time that I discovered that they were blue. Their colour seemed to intensify and brighten as he gazed at Penuel, and I heard him say absently, as though his mind were not quite within his body, "This is my partner, Saginaw. We have shared in the matter of the trees from the beginning."

No one said anything. The Indian stared ahead, without expression as seemed to be a habit with him. My aunt Milhall, with stiffened lips, murmured about laying an extra cover (had they not expected the man to eat?) but Penuel forestalled her. As she went by, I saw Farquharson's eyes follow her, and on his face was the dazed expression of every young man who looked on Penuel. If, I thought, she could only fall in love in her turn, they could marry each other and rent the land; I would have no objection. It would not matter about the judge's mean will if Farquharson had plenty of money. In fact the more I thought about it the more desirable it seemed that Penuel and not myself should become the bride of Farquharson. He did not revolt me; I knew that he was not quite perhaps what is called a gentleman, by which one can mean an idler like my cousin Thornton or someone who lives on credit like my father. Carried away with curiosity and my plans, I craned so far forward to see what was happening next that the two apples shot out of my bodice, bounced from the wooden base of the great baluster down into the hall, and there rolled into the view of all.

"Atalanta," said Mr. Farquharson, who had transferred his gaze upwards. I noted that less than my aunt's grim face, knowing she would pinch and slap me later. I sat frozen, not daring to move or think. At least Farquharson was smiling.

"Apples seem to pursue me," he said. "One fell on my head in the garden today," and at that I had a kindly feeling for him, for he could easily have said that it had been thrown, and thereby probably earned me a whipping. If he would be my ally, it was a great help, as matters stood. The sight of his blunt determined features softened by a smile gave my aunt the cue to smile also, in sickly fashion, as though he were some animal she was trying to lure by saying "Puss, puss, puss." Instead she said aloud "Primrose, come down from there. My niece is a romp, I fear, but it is her age. The plan we discussed will improve her."

What plan was that? I had the sensation of change within and without as I came down the stairs; not gracefully, as Penuel had moved with her skirts hushing, but the reverse, for the green brocade was too long for me and I tripped and would have staggered down the last few steps, except that Farquharson, of whom I was rapidly coming to approve, came forward to help me. I felt his strong grasp land me on my feet in the hall, and by now everyone had turned round, even father. Perhaps it was the first time in my life when I felt of importance, and I had had to spoil it by tripping over the damned skirt. Aunt Milhall made it worse by saying, as though I were in leading-strings, "Now, Primrose, your prettiest curtsy for Mr. Farquharson," and I made a bob and felt a fool. If we had kept company oftener at Pless I should have been more assured in my manners, but there it was. And the amused and helpful expression in Andrew Farquharson's blue eyes as he watched me was nothing, nothing at all, like the look he had given Penuel.

We went in to dinner; I can remember that it was spiced hare. The man Saginaw handled his knife deftly but not in the way we did. I could tell that he was used to eating with his fingers after having used the knife for other things. I thought that I should like to know a great deal more about Saginaw, especially how he had come by his name. I found myself staring at him and was presently aware of the coldly reproving glance of aunt Milhall, and lowered my eyes to my plate. It would be pleasant, after all, to be married and my own mistress, except that perhaps now he had seen Penuel, Mr. Farquharson might change his mind. My innocence of contracts sprang from the fact that I had never yet heard of them, but even I knew that there must have been comings and goings between Arnison, my family, and the tree-planters. In any case there was nothing I could do but wait and see what became of me.

As if to recompense the strangers for my silence, which may have seemed ungracious, aunt Milhall said, in the honeyed voice which was so unlike her daily one that it made me squirm, "It interests me—a mere woman, sirs—to know more of what you propose to do with Pless land. We here, alas, have done less with it than would have been the case had our purses matched our possessions," and I noted not for the first time that she spoke as if Pless belonged to all of them, herself and Thornton and Penuel, whereas it would be true to say that all three of them lodged here at our expense. Mr. Farquharson, on whom no whit of the tale was lost, turned the blue gaze on her.

"You have an interest in Pless, madam? The attorney told me that the land is by direct inheritance and owned by Mr. Tebb," but my aunt, determined not to receive an open snub from one whose social consequence she thought to be less than her own, no matter how much money he had made, put in swiftly "I have kept house here—have I not, James?—since my poor sister-in-law Marjory, Primrose's mother, began to ail, eight years almost to the day it will be. I have been as a mother myself to the poor child, as she lacks her own." This statement was not referred to me for comment, otherwise I do not know what I would have said. Whatever aunt Milhall resembled, it was not my mother. She had turned a look on me which in its amiability was quite foreign, so I put my tongue in my cheek on Andrew Farquharson's side of the table. Whether he noted it or not I shall never know, for once again he had turned his eyes, as though he could not keep them from straying there, to where Penuel sat quietly eating her dinner beside my father. The latter did not eat pleasantly, and as if to atone for the embarrassment of silence Farquharson spoke at length, which I was shortly to find he did seldom.

"There is no secret about what we propose to do, madam; simply in the possession of the seed itself, and the way of growing it. That only I and Saginaw know, and one other."

"Who is the other?" I was so intrigued by the speech that I could not help interrupting; aunt Milhall looked sour and Andrew smiled at me.

"The last chief of the Erie tribe, who were driven from their homeland last century and who bore the seed with them into an alien country, where it would not grow."

He spread out his hands and, seeing us all listening, downed his obvious ardour and said modestly "Truth to tell, it is a tree which should grow very quickly to provide timber for roof-beams and the masts of ships. From the legends—there is nothing else—it should be so large that I have called it the Polyphemus fir, after the giant in classical tales. We may succeed or we may fail, but the ground of Pless seems suitable for growing it. I hope that it will do so profitably and that our agreement may—may bear fruit."

The expressions flitting over my aunt's face were so well worth watching that I was not embarrassed by this last remark. I could almost see her thoughts follow one another, in turn to be considered and then cast off. Well I knew that she would have married me to Thornton had the lands of Pless not been poor, untilled, unprofitable except for its few small farms, and boggy into the bargain, and the house half eaten away with rot and worm and even the furniture taken long ago to pay father's debts. He sat now with his poor head nodding. I do not know if he understood a word of what had been said. For some reason my mind harked back to the time when it had been proposed I marry Thornton, and we had laughed over it together for at that time we had still been friends, and he had said "Marry a bubble-headed chit without a penny to bless herself, and manners like a wildcat? Never I," and I had replied with spirit "Go and get yourself a rich old widow, for no other will look at you; why should they hand their silver to you on a plate when you have none of your own, and are under my aunt's thumb as well?" Then Thornton had stopped laughing and sulked instead, for he hated being made a fool of. I think that was why I had stopped being friends with him.

He was sulking now, for he hated not to be the centre of attention, and though his good looks had thickened and grown coarse with too much wine he could generally command it. In the idle manner he would use to conceal the fact that he was interested despite himself, he said "How did you come by the seeds?" and my aunt surveyed him with pride.

Andrew Farquharson looked at him across the table. No one can tell how he would have answered, for the man Saginaw spoke for the first time, laying down his knife.

"A chieftain of the Lost Tribe gave them to him, for trying to save his son."

It was flatly stated, in careful English, and might have been a remark about the weather.

# *Two*

My Mother and Father had first met one another in Rome, where her father was a Jacobite merchant of cheeses and wines. Since his exile after the 1715 Rising he had grown rich in this way, despite the scorn of many of his compatriots who preferred either to enter the French army or do nothing and starve. Grandfather Goodwin was a prudent man; he did not even marry until he was fifty. There was one daughter of the marriage, and then his wife died. The little girl, Marjory, had the misfortune to catch the smallpox very badly, so that her face was scarred for life. But for the scars she would have been pretty; she had, as I have said already, fine dark eyes with long lashes, and with her father's riches she might have been a sought-after bride. But her affliction made her very shy, and she never went out to balls and assemblies or to any of the gaiety that exiles pursue in their own way; even when walking she wore a veil, and continued solitary. How my father met her, or heard of her, I do not know. Certainly someone must have told him that she was the daughter of a rich merchant who had been exiled for King James.

Father at that time was himself in exile for another reason, namely his creditors, who were so many that a price had even been put on Pless itself, entailed though it might be, but nobody could be found to buy it. My aunt Milhall, who was newly married then, said she could recall bidders coming and tapping at the woodwork, and going away when they found it was full of worm and the grounds poor and marshy. So Pless was saved: but my father, James Tebb—it chanced that he had been christened with a Stuart name, and now it was in his favour—speedily cozened the old merchant into further acquaintance, for Grandfather Goodwin was always hospitable to those who had lost their homes and fortunes in the '15 or the '45, which last was not long gone by. The crowding abroad of escaped Highland gentry had slowed, and so my father was in the less danger of coming across those who had truly fought for Prince Charles Edward. His only accomplice was a man whose name I am glad I do not know, for he was a rascal, and gave father the information he needed. Father came to dinner at Goodwin's house with the tale that he was exiled from his estates because of his services to the Stuart cause, but that, not having fought at Culloden, he was not on the proscribed list and might return to his estates on the payment of a fine. He had been wounded, he said, at Falkirk fight, which had prevented his being at Culloden. It is extraordinary that the shrewd old merchant believed him, and bade him come often to the house. His fine manners and handsome face soon rid my mother of her shyness, and she fell headlong in love with him, being unworldly and hitherto protected from rogues. My father's accomplice did what he might, telling Goodwin and his daughter of the bravery of James Tebb at Falkirk and, moreover, Prestonpans, and on the march to Derby. So things turned out as they were fated to, and presently my father, with suitable modesty, asked the merchant for his daughter's hand in marriage: he could provide for her, he swore, when he was able to return with her to his freed estates.

It was difficult for my grandfather to refuse my mother

anything she had set her heart on, though he grieved at losing her. The pair were married, and by the time they reached Antwerp on the journey back home, mother was pregnant with me and father was spending most of her dowry in the payment of his debts. At least he was able to bring his wife back home for the lying-in to take place at Pless, disappointed though he was that I turned out to be a daughter.

I hope that at any rate I brought my mother some happiness. I can remember when I was very tiny she used to take my hand to help me walk, and would hold me afterwards on her knee by the fire. I cannot believe that she was happy with such a husband, though they say she loved my father to the end. Soon after my birth he ceased to keep up even the appearance of mending his ways, and was in debt again and would be found drunk in bed with farm-girls and inn-women, one of whom gave him the great pox. By the time I was old enough to notice such things it had entered his brain, and had left him paralysed and witless. The physicians said there was nothing to be done; they had dosed him with all the drugs they knew.

When mother died, I can remember my bewildered grief. Shortly before that, while she was ill, aunt Milhall, by then a widow, had taken the housekeeping upon herself and had her fingers already in the larders and in the ledgers. No doubt someone of the kind would have been needed to look after a helpless invalid and a small motherless child, but I always loved Bethia, the servant, best. She would speak to me of my mother and then sing songs to me. I can remember one to this day, which went

> *When we rode down to yon toun*
> *Wew were a comely sight to see;*
> *My love was clad in the black velvet*
> *And I mysel' in cramasie,*

—and though I could not picture Bethia, with her whiskered face, riding down to anywhere at all dressed in crimson beside a young man, I loved the song. There was another about the Queen of Elfland and I recall saying to Bethia, when I would be about eight years old, "But if they rode through red blood to the knee, she'd spoil her green silk skirts."

"It's naught but a song," Bethia said, and did not try to explain. Meantime aunt Milhall and Penuel and Thornton had made themselves at home in Pless, and about the time I made the remark about the Queen of Elfland my aunt contrived the rich marriage for Penuel I have already described. Whatever of her other sins are forgiven aunt Milhall, I do not think that that will be. I only once saw Penuel's ancient bridegroom when he came to marry her; and if cold parsimony and hot lust can combine together in a human countenance, that is what he looked like. I can remember the bridal bed all decked with flowers. After he died Penuel never spoke of him again. Thornton told me later that she had begged and pleaded and wept not to have to marry such a man, but aunt Milhall was adamant; we must repair our fortunes.

Now it was my turn.

# *Three*

Tꜱɪᴍᴇ ᴘʟᴀʏꜱ ᴛʀɪᴄᴋꜱ with memory, and I do not think that that night Andrew Farquharson told us the full story of how he had obtained the seed. He was not, as I have tried to make clear, a person of many words, and the company at table was only half sympathetic. After Saginaw's remark there would be silence, and then perhaps a renewal of polite talk. I do not remember. Nor do I think that it was that same night that Penuel came to my room with her hair unbound, and told me the story. I was sent to bed after dinner, but I did not go straight to sleep: I can recall standing at the window in my night-shift, looking down into the moonlit garden at each familiar shrub and tree made silver-barred and strange. Everything would change still more if the strangers, the man I was to marry and his dark shadow, had their way and came here to dig up the marsh and plant tree-seed. I had neither seen such things done nor heard of them before, but I knew that there would be change at Pless. Now, everything was as I had always known it and as I loved it, and I stood watching till the moon went behind a cloud and I felt cold and climbed into bed, but could not warm myself.

It still seems to me that Penuel glided in then, although she could not have done so that night; more time was needed to hear the tale from Farquharson. But I remember how she came, in her shift and nightgown with her fair hair hanging, and she seemed like a piece of the moonlight and of the garden, perhaps a dryad, who haunted trees. She sat by my bed and talked, talked far into the night, long after I should have been asleep. She had the air of one who tells herself of wonders as well as the listener. It made me think what a silent creature she was in the ordinary way and I remember thinking, as if pursuing my own thoughts, "Even Penuel is going to be changed."

I said then, for it had been preying on me, "Penuel, why do you not marry Mr. Farquharson yourself and use the land? He would far liefer you than me; he could not keep his eyes from you at dinner." Then she cast her gaze down and became prim and withdrawn, and I had to remember that she was Lady Munro who consorted with persons of letters in Edinburgh half the year, and never spoke of remarriage. So I cozened her, as I knew very well how to do, and made her tell me the tale she had come in to tell. The truth was that I wanted to hear it.

Here is the tale. Andrew Farquharson as a boy had run away from home and had taken ship to Canada, where he worked his passage; he was poor then. He had it in mind to be an explorer and trapper, and this meant living half the year in a country far wilder than Pless, where the summer is short and full of flies and the winter long and the snow deep, so much so that men do not go out but dig themselves into a warm firelit hut with supplies, and wait for the spring. But winter is the time when an animal's fur is thickest and so the trappers must do all their killing and pelting in the cold season, then they store the skins and eat dried flesh until the thaw.

Andrew and one old trapper who was teaching him were in their hut by the fire, with the snow blowing hard outside, and they were scraping and scouring beaver skins with sharp flakes of ice. In the midst of this activity they heard a scrabbling at the door. It might have been a dog, or a wolf; Andrew took his gun and went and opened the door, and in out of the blizzard crawled a creature who proved to be a man; a young Indian, almost a boy, gaunt and too weak to stand. He lay on the floor and began to cough in the warmth, and with the coughing came blood.

"Only a boy, and he was dying of consumption, which the Indians fall a prey to easily once they have met white men," said Penuel, her eyes darkening with pity. "Andrew—" I noticed how swift she was to call him Andrew, as though they had always been friends—"Andrew lifted the boy and put him on his own pallet and nursed him, till he was able to speak."

"He might have caught the consumption," I said.

"No doubt he knew that, and risked it. At first they found what they thought was a great thing, and certainly it made Andrew his fortune. On the boy's back were strapped fine beaver skins, much larger and richer than any Andrew had ever seen. So he asked the boy where he came from and where to find such beaver."

"And did the boy tell him?"

Penuel looked down at her hands. "The boy said 'I am the son of the last chieftain of the Lost Tribe, the Cat Indians whose land was laid waste these many years since.' Neither you nor I would know it, but Andrew knew; he said the land had been burned and the men slaughtered by the Iroquois Indians, a century back, and the saying still went *They made a desert and called it peace.* There were only a few of the women and children left, and those who were strong enough to walk left the shores of great Lake Erie where their tribe had always lived, growing crops and spearing fish, for they were not a hunting tribe. They travelled far, far to the north, away from the enemy who would have slain them, but many died on the journey. It was a long journey, long enough for the children to grow to be men.

In the end, they found a valley in the far north-west where no hunting tribes lived, and there they settled and tried to make a new life. They had carried all that time, though the journey took many years, the great secret the Iroquois wanted and never found; the seeds of the Polyphemus fir."

"The ones that will be planted here?" I said curiously. I wondered what was so particular about this tree that the enemy Indians had wanted the seed and gone to such lengths to obtain it. I also wondered afresh how Andrew had done so. Penuel meantime had forgotten her narrative and had leaned over to hug me, having forgotten she was Lady Munro.

"Oh, sweetheart, how glad I am that they will, for your prospects could not be better; you will be able to live in ease and comfort, no longer poor or running wild without a proper education, for Andrew says he will send you to school, and buy Thornton a lieutenancy in the army, which he has always wanted but we could never contrive it."

Armies? Schools? Why had I guessed nothing of it, all this planning? It seemed as if I were to be changed too. Suddenly I wanted the strangers to go away, the coloured man and the white, and leave me to my own devices, to the strange secret places in the untidy shrubbery; to Penuel as she was, and as I loved her. I blurted out "Suppose I refuse to marry him? Can none of this happen then?"

"Darling, you would be very foolish to refuse."

"Well, then, I'm foolish. I'm only twelve years old, and 'tis too young to be married. And I don't want to go to school."

Penuel looked grave. "You have no will in law, I think," she said. "You are a minor, and your guardians could make the contract for you. Why do you not wish to marry Andrew? Have you taken him in dislike? He seems a kind young man, and sober." Penuel did not mean this to be a jest, but I had an impulse to laugh, and then to cry. "It is you he wants to marry," I repeated firmly. "You may be as angry as you like." I was not jealous, I was thinking; but to be married merely for my inheritance of marsh, as though I did not matter, was what hurt. I did not signify, I, Primrose Tebb, who could love and hate as well as anyone. I knew that I did not dislike Andrew Farquharson. Yet he had hardly noticed my existence, except for the matter of the dropped apples. But Penuel—

She had flushed, the colour creeping up over her throat and face like wine, like roses. "I shall not marry again," she said coldly. "Pray do not speak in such a way."

"Then tell me the tale of the dying young Indian." I was anxious to placate her; it was of no use, she would never marry Andrew Farquharson even if he asked her. Briefly, I felt sorry for him. Then I listened to the tale again, and it was so marvellous I forgot my petulance and how important I was to myself.

Andrew had nursed the boy and before the young Indian died, he had told Andrew where to find the great beaver in a lake high in the mountains near the country now inhabited by the surviving tribe. White men had never trapped there, and not even many Indians knew of it. It was very far away. The dying boy also gave a bag he wore about his neck to Andrew, asking him to take it back to his father the chief. It was the precious box of seeds, which he had stolen and thought he could sell for money, to buy whisky and guns. But he had fallen ill after he left the valley and no white man would deal with him when he saw the blood. Andrew was the first who had not been afraid.

How can I describe Andrew's journey to find the lost Erie tribe and the great beaver? He travelled far and long, much of the way alone; the old man who taught him trapping had told him he was a fool, and would leave his bones in the mountains under a snowdrift. He climbed slopes covered in summer with blowing grass and strange herbs, primal rocks that are as old as the world; he heard the thunder of great waterfalls and saw wild beasts he had not dreamed of; lynx, fox, wolf, bear,

marten, beaver. He saw the maples scarlet in autumn and the
birch yellow-green with spring; his journey took many months,
and he had to hunt for his food like the tribes through whose
country he passed; it was fortunate that these were friendly,
but they either could not or would not tell him of the lost
Erie tribe. Most thought them dead years since, wiped out in
the massacre: had it not been for the sick boy he had watched
die at last, Andrew himself might have thought the tale a dream
and have abandoned his quest. But he persevered, as perhaps
only Andrew would have done; and in the end he found the
valley.

The tribe were fearful of him; they had never seen a white
man, and they stopped tending their rows of straggling sun-
flowers to turn and stare. Later, shyly, when they saw he was
friendly, they came closer; he showed them his gun and how it
fired, and let them hold it, and then let them see the bag about
his neck. When they saw that the women set up a wailing and
the gaunt men, by signs, took him to their chief. This very old
man—he might have been fifty, but the tribe had suffered from
long travel and disease, and would not make old bones—had
white hair and a lined face, and when Andrew put the bag
into his hands the tears fell down his cheeks in mourning for
his son. Andrew could tell him nothing in words, but by signs
it was clear what had happened; by evening, all of the tribe
gathered about him, and offered him sunflower cakes to eat,
and fish they had caught in the bay.

He stayed with the tribe for many weeks, as he was weary
and winter was not far away. Slowly—he does things in an
unhurried fashion, and does them well—he learned their
tongue, and could make himself understood by them. It was
plain that the tribe was dying because it had no will to live;
such things can happen, and have done, in history. The women
could not bear children or if they bore them, had no milk; the
men were racked with disease and many of them coughed
blood, like the chief's dead son. One day the old man himself

sent for Andrew and said "Man of the bright hair, we cannot grow our tree in this valley. You would have saved my son; instead, save the tree." And he told Andrew the secrets of planting and nurturing the great fir, which had been handed down to him from his ancestors. Then he gave the seed-box itself back to Andrew, fastening it with his own hands in the bag about Andrew's neck. "Go in peace, stranger," he said, and told him where to find big beaver on his journey.

There is one thing Penuel did not mention to me. When Andrew was coming near to the valley, he saw an arrow shot into a tree. He waited and spread his hands out, to show he was no enemy, and presently a dark man came out of the trees and barred his path. Andrew tried, uselessly, to speak English to him and then, curiously, French. "I do not know what made me think of it," he said to me later. It turned out that the man was an outcast from the tribe; occasionally he visited them and took their women. His mother had been a chieftain's daughter and on the great northward journey, a French trapper had seduced her and got her with child. She lived with him for a time after the child was born and he was called by the place-name of his birth, Saginaw. When he was six years old his mother felt a longing to return to her own people and she left the trapper, who had in any case used her badly and had often beaten her and taken other women. Somehow Morning Star—this was her name—had followed in the way the tribe had taken and had found them, but died soon after. The boy grew up half at enmity, despised by his mother's people and hating his father's. Unlike the tribe he would hunt for meat, and as soon as he was old enough he made his home by himself in the forests. When Andrew asked to be shown the tribe's dwelling-place Saginaw went part of the way with him; when he came back, after many months, Saginaw accompanied him and was his guide to the country of the great beaver. They trapped all that winter and when spring came, Andrew took Saginaw with him to the south parts where the auctions were held, going part of the way by land and part by water, with birch-leaves bound round their heads to keep away the flies.

The great pelts fetched much money in the market. Andrew knew that if he could find a white man who would be his partner, someone he could trust, he could lay a route between the trapping country and the auctions and send yearly harvests of great skins. He found his man; he was a kinsman of the old trapper who had told Andrew he was a fool to try to find the Cat Indians in their new country, or to hunt for big beaver.

That is the story as I heard it, and the words I have used are only those I know. To have been there, to have taken part in the trapping and the portages and auctions, to watch oneself grow rich, cannot be spoken of in so short a space. But Andrew had indeed grown rich; and after some years spent in learning and perfecting his fur-trading, he had come home to find himself a place to plant the fabled tree. There was primal rock in this land too. He knew it should be possible to grow the fir as well here as in Canada, watching and caring for it daily as he knew how to do. And so he had come to Pless, and I was thrown into the bargain. The best thing to do with me at present was to send me away to school, though I did not agree; but then no one asked me concerning it.

# Four

THE FACT THAT my marriage had been agreed upon by the adults could be seen by the speed with which the two men, white and brown, went to work. I had never before seen an acquaintance, who had dined at our table, take off his coat and dig in his shirt-sleeves; at the beginning, like aunt Milhall, I was somewhat shocked. But it had already been made known to me that I was not, after all, marrying a gentleman; some allowance had to be made for the lack of dowry except Pless land, which well-born people found too poor to be of interest.

It was not so now. Within a week all the boggy part had been dug into trenches, the turned sods shining with their marsh-slime in the fitful sun, which dried them soon. The trenches were not parallel but radiating from a centre. Afterwards Andrew put lime upon them, turning the field into a jumbled fantasy of patterned white and brown. He himself was covered in the white dust and washed himself afterwards at the pump in the yard. The Indian, further off, was naked to the waist and did not wash himself. He worked as hard as Andrew, but seldom came near the house. They had built themselves a hut of cut logs and peat-sods, and Saginaw had begun to light

37

a fire and cook his meals there. The hut was near the centre of what would be the plantation.

I saw all this because I would watch from the orchard, or from my window when I was left in peace. One day, aunt Milhall being absent on some errand of her own, I stole over to look at the field from close at hand. Andrew was, as usual, working nearby in his shirt-sleeves and had taken off his stock. The back of his neck showed freckled beneath his tied hair, and when he turned round to greet me I could see the top of his exposed chest; it, too, was covered with a light-coloured fuzz of hair. I had never before seen a man so nearly unclad. It did not seem to trouble him; he laid down his spade, wiped the sweat from his eyes with his arm, and grinned shyly. So solid and real a presence was he that the whole fantastic tale of the finding of the seed seemed, by contrast, unreal. Yet it must be true; they were working hard enough to prove it.

"What are you doing?" I said, foolishly, but we had had few direct words with one another. I went on with more intelligence. "Why are the furrows dug in such a way, and not in straight lines?" For I had seen farmers ploughing, on the few outlying farms that remained to Pless, and I saw that this method was quite different. Nor were there sea-gulls swooping down to get what they could from the furrows; the land was too sour.

He showed no irritation at my presence, though he must have disliked to be interrupted at his work. He answered pleasantly "To tell you that would be to tell you a part of the secret of the tree. Can you keep secrets, Primrose?"

I thought over the matter and then said I could. As it happened there was no one to whom I could have told a secret, except Bethia and Penuel. Perhaps he would not mind if Penuel knew. I gathered my courage, then asked him. He turned away and looked out over the worked sods and said "No, I do not mind if Lady Munro knows of it; but only she, and no other."

Then he had not told Penuel, I was thinking. I felt of some importance now that my future husband was telling me a secret first. I traced a pattern on the limed earth with my shoe, and stared at the little dark line it made. Then I looked up at Andrew again. He had brought out something from the bosom of his shirt where it hung on a strip of leather. It was a small bag, and opening it he showed me a large shiny seed-case, dark brown in colour and polished with age.

"That is what the chief gave you?"

"That is the eye of Polyphemus: the seed-box which may make our fortune, and contains many seeds. You may hold it if you wish. Mark it well, for if you ever see another, we have succeeded. Only one grows in the end, from a queen tree, and it takes five years to mature. That is why the trenches radiate; when we find the queen, she must be re-planted in the centre of the forest where she is under our eyes day and night. It would be easy, once word ran round, for a thief to come, otherwise, and take the seed. So either I or Saginaw will keep watch, and we will perhaps have a dog to tell us if strangers come. Now I have told you part of the secret; remember your promise."

"Does the queen tree look like the rest?" I was fascinated; it sounded like a hive of bees. "No," he said, "she is larger, and her leaves are more bronze in colour. It will be easy to find her when she is young, and we will take her carefully, at the right time of year, to where we may watch over her. The trees take eight years to reach their full height. By that time you will be twenty years old."

I laughed; it seemed a long time ahead. I held the seed-box in the palm of my hand and stroked its surface, and thought of the chief's young son who had stolen the seeds and run far away from his place of exile to find whisky and guns. "If this seed is so old," I said, "how do you know that it will grow at all? Perhaps it has died," but I could feel that it had not; there was a warmth about the box which came partly from Andrew's skin, but partly again from a life-force, which I knew was within it. He smiled, did not reply, and took it from me.

I turned away, and looked at Saginaw, who was labouring
in another part of the field, his back shining with sweat and
the muscles upon it lithe as an animal's. Well, I thought, he
was part Cat Indian; not a tame cat that sat by a fire, but a
great fierce wild one, which moves in silence and then pounces
on its prey. I shivered suddenly. "Are you cold?" said Andrew.
"Best return to the house; you have no wrap."

I ignored that, as he in his turn had ignored my question
about whether the seed would grow. "Why do you like
Saginaw?" I said bluntly. "It is—strange that you should be
friends," and then I felt that I had been impudent, as aunt
Milhall constantly told me I was, and waited for a rebuff. It
did not come. "We are blood-brothers," said Andrew gently.
"No man was Saginaw's friend till he met me. After he had
shown me the great beaver country we cut our wrists and laid
them together so that the blood mingled, and swore to plant
the seed together and not abandon it or one another till it grew.
We could not stay in Canada for this; there would be a great
desire among the Indians to steal the seed for themselves, and
this may even happen here, at Pless, when the news spreads.
So keep silence, Primrose." He smiled, and I knew he trusted
me. Suddenly he frowned. "Do not fret yourself that if we fail,
we will be poor," he said. "I have told your father and your
aunt this and now it is right that I tell you. Whether or not the
trees grow you will not suffer. If they grow, we will make a
fortune from the wood for ships. If they do not, we have an
income from the beaver each year. I have shown the way to a
trusted few, and they will continue to bring down the big fine
skins that we know of and others do not. As long as men wear
beaver hats, we won't starve, or want for necessities."

He waited to return to his digging, and I knew I wearied
him, but there was a great deal I wanted to ask him and if
they were sending me off to school, there might not be the
chance again. "You were poor once," I said. "Tell me of that."

"Poor? Ay; my father was a dominie in the Highlands, a schoolmaster as you would call it down here, and they are not well paid. He wanted me to follow in his footsteps, but I had other notions, and when he died I ran away. He had given me a good education, with the French language and Latin and Greek."

He was fingering the spade and I knew now how he had know nabout such subjects as Atalanta: I happened also to know the story of that lady and her apples, because now and again in my childhood I had had a governess, but they never stayed long. I said now, apropos of nothing "The young man threw apples at Atalanta, not she at him."

"I stand corrected."

"I wish you could marry Penuel. I would be willing for you to use the land and you could pay me back when you had made your fortune. Then I needn't go to school."

He did not reply about land, school, or fortunes; he had turned to his digging again and I saw the colour flood his freckled skin as it had done Penuel's, when I asked her the same thing. He said over his shoulder "A man does not marry a goddess," and I tossed my hair out of my eyes and turned and left him, for some reason in a worse temper than when I had come out.

# *Five*

OTHER CHANGES came to Pless. First of all my cousin Thornton
left to join his regiment, near to bursting from pride of himself
in the pair of colours Andrew had bought him through the
influence of an Edinburgh friend of Penuel's. This had the
advantage that her brother might be quartered near her in the
capital. His going left no gap: after he had ridden away I
was left thinking how little I missed him. We had dealt well
enough together all our lives, and had been in brief collusion
to prevent our marriage to one another at the time it was
suggested. But now Thornton was no loss to me and I only
reflected how he had become so lazy that life in the army would
perhaps be good for him. No doubt Andrew had had this same
thought. The only way Thornton might be missed was by
reason of the aid he gave my father, helping him in and out
of his chair and sometimes seeing to his bodily needs. This task
Andrew took upon himself, leaving the Indian to guard the
field. I recall that my aunt Milhall was shocked, and bridled
as she was sometimes wont to do now that we were less poor.

"Cannot a servant be hired to deal with him?" she asked,
sounding as if it had been another servant to whom she spoke,

and concerning some animal and not her own brother. Andrew raised his head from where he was bending over my father and I could see that his eyes showed very blue. "We have enough money to live, ma'am, but not to squander," he told her. "Primrose is to have an education and your son is provided for. Moreover, as you already know, you yourself are welcome to stay on under this roof as long as it shall suit you."

I could have laughed in her face; he had hit out shrewdly, making it evident that he was well aware aunt Milhall and her family lived off us at Pless. But it would be as well if aunt were to stay on here, with Bethia, instead of troubling her daughter. Penuel did not love her mother, and at the least, out of her sorry marriage, had earned the right to be mistress of her own house in Edinburgh. Had my aunt settled there, the ordering would have been in her hands within the hour.

Penuel was no longer at Pless; she had left at the same time as Thornton, so that he could visit her when he had leave. She would return for my wedding, which was to take place before I went to school. In this way also it was necessary for my aunt to remain at Pless; had she not been there, it would not have been proper for me to remain at Pless with only the men and the servant. I need not say that it was aunt Milhall herself who pointed this out; such matters seldom occurred to me.

I myself was preoccupied less by thoughts of my wedding than that afterwards I was to leave Pless and be sent to school in Edinburgh. One comfort was that Penuel would be near; we would be separated only by the length of the Royal Mile, for my school for young ladies was in the Lawnmarket. I had been intrigued when they told me this and had asked if lawn was still sold in the market, and Penuel had smiled and said all manner of things were sold there, in the booths and the little arcades over which town-houses hung. This consoled me some little for having to go away, but before Penuel left I had wept against her.

"I don't want to go," I said dismally. "Must I go, Penuel?

It is only Andrew who thought of it, and we needn't heed him, now that he has got the land."

"Andrew is kind enough to have paid for your board there, so I believe you must be grateful to him."

"Why may I not live with you? I could travel the mile each day in a coach."

Penuel smiled and said that she did not keep a coach, but took a sedan-chair when she wanted to travel up the town. "In any case, as you know, I am not in Edinburgh all of the year."

"Then you will be at Pless here with Andrew, and I shall not. Oh, Penuel—"

She frowned and I bit my lip. I had promised not to mention my thought again that she would be better to marry Andrew than I. In any case the stuff for my wedding-dress was bought, which made the matter final.

I can remember what else Penuel said. "Andrew wants to see you turned into a young lady, with polite manners and accomplishments."

"I shan't need accomplishments at Pless."

She shook her fair head gently. "They serve to divert the mind, Primrose, as well as pleasing others. You will never be lonely if you have learned to play and sing, and draw and paint, and dance as they do at assemblies, and love poetry and maybe speak a foreign language. I believe they teach French very well at the young ladies' school."

"I shan't be going to France."

"You never know where you may be going, as the wife of a rich forest-owner and fur-trader. Why not think of how lucky you are?" But I scowled and would not be comforted. Nevertheless it was reasonable to send me to school, as Andrew himself had told us he would have to travel now and again to London, or even perhaps to Canada to oversee the affairs of his beaver-skin company. Would that leave only the Indian to look after father? No one knew.

Something happened then which was not a part of the plan; aunt Milhall died. I do not know what was wrong with her and neither did the physician. One evening she ate her dinner heartily, as usual, and later went up to bed and was found dead there in the morning. It was Andrew who told me, gently as if he felt that I would grieve for her. Then "We must send for Lady Munro," he said, as if he were half unwilling that Penuel disturb him again.

I was glad; hiding my gladness through all the days of mourning and the funeral, which was a quiet affair as my aunt had few friends living. I knew that now, when I came home to Pless for the holidays, Penuel must accompany me as chaperon, and this made me very happy. I loved Penuel better than anyone in the world; better than my father, certainly better than the man who was to be my husband. And, I told myself wryly, he loved Penuel too.

# Six

ON THE MORNING of my wedding day I looked out of the window and saw the rain drizzling down, and outside Andrew and the Indian, sleeves rolled above the elbow and shoes thick with mud, hauling great vats to try to catch the water. They did not see me and I recalled a conversation I had had with Andrew the previous day, which displeased me.

"You will not touch the orchard?" I had said. He smiled and promised that the trees and shrubs should be left as they were "though perhaps if there is time, we will prune them." This sent desolation through me, but Andrew's next statement was worse. "The little stream, I fear, will have to go. We must divert it to irrigate the trees when they appear."

I did not know what irrigation was, but the loss of the brook would be a disaster; all the primroses would vanish from the place where my mother had sat and thought of my name before I was born. I stared at Andrew's unfeeling face and for the first time hated him. He might have brought prosperity to Pless, but I should finish by hating it also, so changed would it be by the time he had done. But it was of no use to say anything; how could the will of a twelve-year-old girl prevail? Aunt

Milhall had scolded me so often for being forward and pert
that by now I was not forward enough; I have no doubt that
Andrew might have tried to save the stream had I explained
why I felt about it as I did.

I turned back into the room and surveyed my wedding
dress, laid out already on the chest. Penuel had chosen the
stuff in Edinburgh. It was both pretty and hard-wearing,
being damson-coloured with stripes of cherry, and with a wide
white lawn collar and cuffs at the sleeve-elbows. There was a
matching cherry ribbon to thread through my hair. I could
wear the gown on great occasions at school. The thought did
not lift my spirits.

Penuel came soon to dress me. She had herself washed my
hair the previous day and it was soft as silk. She combed it
becomingly, coaxing the curls into court-fashion although they
would never grow long enough. "May I use your rouge?" I
asked, and she smiled and said "No, on no account. You look
as charming as I have ever seen you. I hope Andrew will be
pleased." So she had dressed me for Andrew, not for myself.
I was on the way to becoming a sullen bride, but Penuel said
"Come and help me lace," and that lifted me out of my ill-
humour. She was wearing the lilac dress which became her, not
having bought herself anything new; after all we were both in
half-mourning for aunt Milhall.

Carriages had begun to arrive and we went downstairs at
last to meet our few neighbours who had assembled, some from
long distances. There was the Admiral who never visited,
stationed for once in his full-bottomed wig behind my father's
chair; he tried to talk to father, but the white witless face
nodded always and made no reply. Otherwise the company
was the same as at aunt Milhall's funeral, and it struck me
that this was hardly more joyful an occasion, although more
cheerful than Penuel's, for at least my bridegroom was under
thirty and not mean. I was the youngest person present by far;
there were hardly any young people in the country round Pless,

except the children of the tenant-farmers. Everyone of interest had gone long ago, in pursuit of money or pleasure, to Edinburgh or London. I thought it a dull scene, when there entered my bridegroom and Saginaw, who was bridesman.

I was pleased to see that Andrew had atoned for his rough appearance earlier that day by making himself very elegant. I had a notion of such matters from Thornton, who fancied fine clothes and could never have them before he had gone, gloriously arrayed, into the army in tasselled boots and powder. Andrew wore nothing of this kind, but his linen was spotless, though it was plain. He wore a dark coat and grey breeches, and his hair had a gloss on it from pomade. Few of the company wore powder at this hour. I was pleased enough with my bridegroom and he, judging from his expression as he came to take his place by my side, was pleased enough with me; or was it with Penuel, standing behind me as my brideswoman?

Father was pitiful. It had been decided that if I stood by his chair with Andrew by me, and the clergyman, father could give me away. But he hardly understood what was expected of him and the touch of his puffed dough-white hand made me shiver. However the ceremony proceeded, the clergyman standing by the hearth with his book and bands. A beam of sunshine struck through one of the windows and someone said "Happy is the bride the sun shines on" and others "'Tis shame, and such a child!" and everyone kissed me, Andrew with a dry peck on my cheek, but his grasp of my other hand was firm and strong and the ring was on my finger.

Saginaw as I have said was bridesman. The clothes he wore were respectable by his standards and he had even brought a hat. I knew the custom was that the bridesman and brideswoman should kiss also, but had supposed it would not happen in this case. How mistaken I proved to be! Before anyone could prevent it Saginaw had seized Penuel and kissed her long and hard on the mouth, keeping his arms round her as if he would never let her go. I do not know how many people noticed as they were beginning by then to pass round the cake and wine. But *I* had noticed, and saw also that when the Indian released Penuel at last, so suddenly that she staggered back, her mouth seemed bruised by a great red mark on the skin.

I felt angry with Andrew for choosing so unsuitable a bridesman. But he had little choice; Thornton might have done, but he could not obtain leave again so soon after his mother's funeral. And after all a blood-brother would, I dared say, serve.

Into what alien world had I been married? And now I was Primrose Farquharson. The marriage was not to be consummated yet, and soon now I should be taken away to school. I almost welcomed it.

## Seven

I HAD NEVER before been in Edinburgh, and after the coach-journey I was not too tired to look with some eagerness up the long narrow street as it climbed towards the Castle, so grand on its rock, where Thornton was quartered with his regiment. Somewhere among the tall grimy buildings was my school, and my heart sank a little. It seemed difficult to breathe the air here; everywhere was smoke and dirt, the smells of fish and of refuse, and thronging people. But I was to spend two days with Penuel first at her house, and she promised that on the morrow we would walk out and she would show me the sights of the town. It was a jumble of history, she told me, adding that there was talk of draining the great Nor' Loch and building a new clean city joined to the old by bridges. But it had not been started yet.

Penuel's house itself was cold and stark. The maid-servant who opened to us did not smile beneath her starched cap, and even Penuel herself had grown formal, as if the chill place took all warmth from her. Could this be the same Penuel who at home, at Pless, would go off by herself for the whole day plant-hunting, missing her dinner, with her head in a kerchief and old shoes on her feet? She had become one of the tight-laced powdered folk who walked these streets with small affected steps or were carried up and down them in chairs for public hire. Even her voice seemed different, artificial and aware of itself. If I said to her "Now you are Lady Munro" she might pretend not to understand. So I kept silent.

When I was shown my room I was still cold, but the bed seemed soft, with a mattress of down. The covers and curtains were all of printed India muslin, very fine. On the wall hung a portrait of Penuel's late husband in his judge's robes and I looked at his mean mouth and cold eyes and determined to turn my back on him that night. Perhaps Penuel could not bear to have the portrait in her own room. I had heard some-where, I did not remember where, that he had been angry with her for giving him no son.

Next day I saw the sights, as Penuel had promised: the Royal Mile and the Grassmarket, Holyrood and Greyfriars and the windy Nor' Loch with the exquisite little chapel at its eastern end. More than all these I was intrigued by the sight of stay-boned ladies in high wigs with a ship or a wreath of flowers and corn on top, lifting their petticoats aside from the mud of the gutters and talking to one another in high unnatural voices. Once a gust of wind snatched off a lady's ship and her servant, who was walking behind, had to rescue the plunging galleon amid his mistress's genteel screams that she was undone. I began to laugh and Penuel reproved me. "It is not good manners to stare," she said. "It might happen to anyone."

I had begun to feel unhappy. Several of the upholstered ladies greeted Penuel and began to make affected talk with her; they ignored me although she made my name known to them. I began to long for Pless and Andrew and even Saginaw. Looking at Penuel now it was impossible to believe that the dark man had embraced her and left a mark on her mouth. I dared not remind her, or speak of it. I looked at her in her fashionable dress of fine grey stuff, with its padded hips and lawn fichu drawn high about the neck—Penuel was never immodest—and her little hat set on her high-piled hair, and thought "Lady Munro, widow of the judge." We were tired with walking by then and returned to the cold house.

Next day I was taken to school, Penuel accompanying me. She always did her duty.

# Eight

THE SCHOOL ITSELF, being very exclusive, occupied three of the upper floors of one of the old towered buildings in the Lawnmarket, where the quality still dwelt; the greater one's social consequence, the further one had to climb. Later I was to find that from certain of its windows which looked away from the squalid street, one could glimpse green hills and the blue Forth. For the present, however, totally subdued, I was conducted, with Penuel by me, at the heels of a red-cheeked maidservant to the receiving-room. Here the headmistress, Mrs. McLehose, awaited us with a dish of tea, as was her polite custom.

It is beyond my powers fully to describe Mrs. McLehose. At first, despite my shyness, I came close to bursting with suppressed giggles at that interview. Penuel having told me already that it was rude to stare, I thankfully looked at the carpet; but the gentility of Mrs. McLehose's accents were then even more apparent, and I held my breath and tried to think of something sad, which is the best way I know to prevent oneself from laughing. It appeared that Mrs. McLehose's function at the school, and no doubt also in life, was to dispense genteel behaviour. She held her cup with her little finger extended, and made polite exchanges with Penuel in so strong a quintessence of all I had already noted about Edinburgh society that one could hardly follow what she said, especially as she was impeded by a set of china teeth.

"Leedy Munro"—the bow on her bonnet wobbled with the emotion of pronouncing a title—"I hope that the tea is to yer taste." Penuel said that it was, and the lady's broad bosom, which boasted a cameo, expanded as she took what breath her stays permitted. "Perhaps efter, ye will partake of a gless of ratafia?" Penuel refused gently; it was too early in the day. I memorised the carpet-pattern, and listened with half an ear to the continuing abuse of the good Scots tongue; with any luck, I could give an imitation of this self-styled lady when I got back to Pless. I remembered then that there was hardly anyone left at Pless, and felt desolation creep in on me again. Then I remembered that Thornton was here at the Castle. Perhaps one day soon I should see Thornton, and make him laugh with my rendering of Mrs. McLehose.

That personage had briefly turned her attention to me, and said I had a good head of hair. "And her attainments?" she said in a manner which I cannot imitate. Penuel looked at me, and I answered for myself that I knew very little, never having had a governess who stayed long. The bow on the bonnet trembled indulgently. "Veergin soil, indeed! We will make a young leedy of her by the time she has been here two years. It is extraordinary that she is mairrit."

Penuel explained some of the circumstances of my marriage. It turned out that Andrew had arranged for me to have dancing and water-colour lessons, which were extra. This predisposed the headmistress in my favour, and as Penuel prepared to depart I was swept under Mrs. McLehose's well-plumed wing as she prepared to take me to the schoolrooms. I felt gloom rush up at me like a shower of gutter-mud: I clung to Penuel as if I might never see her again.

"Take heart, darling," she whispered, "remember that you are to spend Saturdays with me." This indeed was a ray of light, and I could look forward to it.

When Penuel had gone—I committed the error of going to the window to try to wave her farewell, and was admonished, because it was not ladylike—I was handed over to the lesser luminary of the establishment, who in fact did most of the work; Mrs. McLehose's unmarried sister, Miss Crindle. There was a third sister who saw to the housekeeping and directed the maids. The latter slept (I did not find this out immediately) under the kitchen table.

There were twelve young ladies at the school; I made the thirteenth, which might have caused me some reflection. Of the others, all—I had heard Mrs. McLehose boast of it to Penuel—were proficient in French, Italian, the harpsichord, the globes, needlework, grammar, and polite talk. So much awe had been inspired in me at the thought of meeting these learned damsels that I very nearly vanished downstairs and out into the street. However we found them—Miss Crindle stayed till I was made known—with their faces pressed to the glass in the manner I had just been forbidden, watching what went on in the Lawnmarket, and especially the departure of Penuel's chair. Miss Crindle clapped her hands, and informed them in strident tones what they ought to be at, and were not. This cheered me, and when we were left alone I took a look at them from beneath my lashes. Most were my own age or thereabouts. I noticed particularly a slim girl with black hair and eyes and a pale mischievous face, whose name I must early have been told was Mary Cantlie. She came over soon, clustering about me with the others, as schoolgirls always will for a new inmate; it is at this stage that they decide whether one is to be accepted or tormented.

"You were lucky," said Mary to me later, "because you're pretty. When Isabella came"—(Isabella Campbell had spots) "we called her Raisin Pudding and led her a terrible life, putting chamber-pots in her bed and all the rest. The beds have fleas; you won't escape them, no one does. We sleep four to a bed."

I hoped that I was not to share a bed with Raisin Pudding, and in a short time I had made arrangements, or Mary had, to have me put in her own. The other two occupants were quiet souls who would have made trouble for nobody, including themselves; but Mary and I were devils, and got up to every trick we could think of, night and day. I think we only escaped dire punishment because Mary was second cousin to a duchess.

It was true about the fleas. When I went to visit Penuel on the Saturday, the first thing I asked for was a hip-bath.

There is little more to say about the school. It was no more and no less pretentious than many like it, and the food might have been worse. The fact that I was a married lady obtained me some degree of freedom and caused much comment. Mary was frank.

"Has he done it yet? Everyone wants to know."

I was puzzled. "Done what?" If I had thought for moments, I should have known; I had grown up watching dogs and cattle, and I knew why father was ill. But it had hardly crossed my mind that one day Andrew and I would have to become husband and wife in truth, and the prospect seemed so unlikely that I said haughtily "It is not your concern," leaving Mary in open-eyed wonder for instants before she slapped back, in her sharp way, "I'll wager he hasn't. You're much too small." I said nothing and she thought I must be sulking, and she tried to cozen me. "You're fortunate, at any rate, in that you won't have to be brought out and taught how to try and catch a husband, because you have one already. The assemblies are so stupid, and the eligible men up here are always lawyers, because everyone else has gone to London. Even the nobility aren't here any more. There was one old duke who used to sell evening gloves at the door, they say, but I think he must be dead."

I was glad that the subject of my marriage had been shelved, but I had forgotten the other eleven inmates. The least detail about Andrew intrigued them for days. What colour were his eyes? What colour was his hair? Did he wear a wig? Was he tall, rich, handsome, the heir to a title?

I told them Andrew was seven feet tall and had a squint in both eyes and one was blue and one was brown, and he had seven wigs on stands, one for every day of the week, and he was so rich I could wear silk gowns as often as I liked, but chose not to. Some little time elapsed before the slower-witted ones perceived that I was leading them on a string, and after that it became a popular game to excel in descriptions of my husband. Diversion was rare; both the drawing-master and the dancing-master were unexciting beings, and my fantasies about Andrew at least passed the time.

Smells prevailed. Raisin Pudding had an unfortunate body-odour as well as her spots, and washing was cramped. There was an ancient nobleman living in the top storey, well past the time of life when it might have been hoped that he would propose for an inmate of the school. Daily at eleven o'clock, when we should have been at our lessons, he would venture downstairs to empty his slops in the street. It was a feat of daring to escape whatever we were supposed to be doing and slip out to waylay him, then run giggling away. I saw him myself as often as anyone. He wore a faded turban and a coat which must once have been very splendid, strawberry velvet richly ornamented with silver. By now it was stiff with grease and dirt, and on the one occasion I saw him in a wig it crawled with lice.

"It can't be helped in a town," said Mary airily. "At home we are quite different. If only there were more diversion here! We can't go out walking without old Crindle, and the assemblies when they start again will be very dull and common; anyone can get in, they aren't exclusive."

"Do we all go to them?" I asked. I thought that I should like to see an assembly.

"Not until old McLehose says we are *leedylike* enough and know where to put our feet. I could dance long before I came here. At home we had a master who was much better than this fool now," and her withering glance surveyed the spindly shanks of poor old Mr, McDade, who came weekly to put us through quadrilles and the minuet. "To think he's almost the only man we ever see, except in St. Giles's if you dare look round!" hissed Mary. I said nothing. I had already looked round in church and had seen one or two officers from the Castle, very grand in regimentals and prepared to wink at me; but none of them was Thornton.

When Christmas came I spent it with Penuel. Nobody else in the capital heeded it as the Scots ignore Christmas in order to make themselves extremely drunk at Hogmanay, as they call the new year. Even by then I was still on holiday, and lay late in bed of a morning, staring at the mean old judge on the wall and listening to the chatter and fish-cries in the streets. It was odd to be cheek by jowl with a royal palace while nearby a woman in a black shawl cried cockles for sale. I had no doubt that if I lived long enough in this jumble of an old capital city I should know it and like it, perhaps, but never love it. The folk and the climate were too cold for me; I longed for Pless. I would try to persuade Penuel to take me there in the spring.

I stretched and yawned, and put my tongue out at the judge as I did each morning, and began to think of rising soon and putting on the warm sheepskin slippers Penuel had brought me as a Christmas gift. I had given her in return a brooch, shaped like a heart, which I had found in one of the booths when, as usually happened, she took me shopping on Satur-

days. The brooch was old and looked black till one breathed
on it and rubbed it hard on a surface such as a carpet, when it
showed silver. I had contrived it out of my pin-money without
Penuel seeing, and when I gave it her she was surprised and
pleased. She fastened it in her bodice and wore it every day,
and I said "In the spring holiday, you will be wearing it at
Pless." I never let her forget that that was what I wanted, but
she seemed to hesitate. My young heedless mind had forgotten
the Indian and that she might be afraid of him. There was only
one thing uppermost with me: I should be glad to go home.

## *Nine*

PLESS HAD NOT ALTERED as much as I had feared. I strained forward in the carriage so that I might be the first to see it between the young green of spring birches. The old tower still crumbled, the Restoration front, that had been added in the brief prosperity of a Tebb ancestor, still flaked its plaster. Beyond the tower was the tumbledown wing where my room stood, and beyond again the apple-tree; had Andrew left me that in his diverting of the stream?

But the wonder came when I was at last in the room, and heard the familiar rustle of owls above me in the roof; they had always nested there. I went to the window (the apple-tree was still there, and thick with buds) and looked beyond, to where the marsh had been. There was the miracle; an orderly thin fuzz of brightest green. The Polyphemus fir seeds had taken root, almost every one. I felt glad for Andrew's sake. He had worked hard to prepare for the trees.

I tried to say how pleased I was, when I saw him as he came in at the end of the day, but found myself stammering. He looked tired, I thought, for once noticing another before myself. Outwardly he was the same as ever, grave, preoccupied, homely, busy, courteous; I thought of the words as though from a list of adjectives Miss Crindle had made us copy at school, and realised I was seeing them borne out in real life, from which I had lately seemed removed. With Penuel it was different; as soon as he set eyes on her Andrew's own would light up. I shrugged off my hurt, which would have meant more to me had Andrew been a handsome nobleman six feet tall, such as Mary would have admired. I did not perhaps need to trouble myself about this ordinary man; after all I was fonder of Penuel than of my husband. It was only that my vanity suffered a trifle; Andrew told me I had grown, and then took small heed to me.

He was kind, however. The day after our arrival he led round a pony. "We use them now for hauling the vats in dry weather," he said. "You will find him biddable. Lady Munro says she does not care to ride, so you must go alone."

I did not mind; I knew Penuel was somewhat afraid of horses, and preferred her walking and plant-finding. Daily, after that, I went out by myself on the pony, which was black with a white blaze on his forehead. Some say blacks have too uncertain a temper to be an easy ride, but this was the sweetest ever foaled. I called him Pleasance. Each morning I would be up early, unlike my city self, and would go round to the stables and saddle and bridle Pleasance for our ride. I would be back, hungry, in time for my dinner; but truth to tell I saw little enough of my husband, Penuel, or Saginaw. The latter still cooked his own food and slept in the hut at the centre of the trees, although it had not yet been decided which was the queen fir.

Things fell out as they did for this reason. The holiday was not long, but one day I felt ill and my head ached, and did not ride out. The next day I was as covered in spots as poor Raisin Pudding. The physician was brought, and looked at me; he said it was measles. This disease, which everyone laughs at, can leave singular discomforts behind it; for some weeks after the spots had gone, it affected both my hearing and my sight. I was pleased, as it had happened near the end of the holiday and meant I need not go back to school at present. Less happily, I could not ride Pleasance for the time, being as shaky as an old woman when I finally left my bed. During the time I had been ill Penuel constantly came to see me, for she had had the disease as a child. Andrew, who had not, never came near, but sent kindly messages and once some fruit which he had fetched from the market and which had cost a good deal, no doubt, at that time of year.

I was troubled about Penuel; she was more than usually quiet and withdrawn, and her colour came and went like a young girl's. I wondered if she were in love with Andrew. What a pity it was that neither of them had heeded my suggestions that they marry one another, and rent the land! It was too late now. I said nothing to Penuel, having that much wisdom at any rate; she was kindness itself to me, and used to read to me to save my sore eyes. When I grew well enough to go out of doors we would take short walks together; the spring days were lengthening and turning to summer. The firs had grown notably since I had been in bed.

"Let us go round the plantings, and see them all," I said one day. She looked away, and flushed. "It is too far for you," she said. "You are not well enough yet."

Day by day she put me off with this excuse, and one fine day when the sun was shining I marched towards the radial trenches and said that I, at any rate, was going if she would not; Penuel had no choice but to follow.

One thing comes chiefly to mind about the course of that walk. We had viewed and admired the strong little trees, which were by now almost a foot high. Penuel was pleased, because she had found a bog-plant which had somehow survived the diggings and lime, and we were making our way homeward by the road we had first taken. There were some logs lying in a pile; they were the remains of trees which had been uprooted when the plantings began, and were slowly being chopped into logs for firewood for the house and hut. By them the Indian stood, making water. He did not stop or turn away as he saw us. I felt the blood rush to my face; I had never before seen a man's private parts. Shame and amazement filled me, but as I turned away, not looking at Penuel, I knew that the Indian's black opaque eyes stared on at our retreating backs, without expression. I felt Penuel's steps quicken; she had said nothing. Once we were out of earshot I said, inadequately, "The vulgar savage! He might have fastened his buttons as we went by. Bethia says he has fathered babies on half the farm-women."

Penuel did not answer, and looking at her I saw she was white enough to faint, then colour came flooding back into her cheeks in two bright patches of outrage. The picture of the dark man with his member pissing out its arched jet of urine would not leave me as soon as I wished. I thought of complaining to Andrew, then left the matter; it was after all a natural need, and the man had not known we were about.

Penuel went straight to her room when we returned and did not come down for dinner, so Andrew and I were alone. We talked of his coming journey to London, which he must shortly make to see a consignment of great beaver skins to auction.

On our next walk Penuel overturned her ankle. It happened among last year's dry bracken, and she had not seen a loose stone. I was ahead, and started at her cry of pain; I went back and helped her to regain her balance, but when she put her foot to the ground it hurt her, and was soon badly swollen.

I did not know where to go for help; rain was beginning to fall and we were still some distance from Pless. The only thing to do—I felt an unwillingness I could not take time to explain to myself, for it must be done—was to take Penuel to the nearby forest hut to rest, while I went back for the pony and help from Andrew, if he could be found. It seemed a long and difficult business, and I hoped Saginaw was nowhere near. I recalled Bethia's scornful words about the way he spent his time. Perhaps he would be away, with one of his farm-women.

Somehow, supporting her weight on my shoulder, I got Penuel to the hut, and drew a breath of thankfulness; there was nobody inside. A low fire of peats smouldered on the hearth, with a steaming cooking-pot by it that smelled of herbs. I laid Penuel down on the pallet of birch twigs and bracken that lay against the wall. She was shivering. "I will go to fetch help," I said. "I will make haste, Penuel." I put my cloak over her to keep her warm. She had lain down without protest, her face drawn with pain. I loosed her shoe gently and prepared to leave her.

As I straightened from my task a shadow darkened the doorway against the falling rain. My eyes met the Indian's; as usual, his glance held no feeling. I tried to speak with authority. "Lady Munro has hurt her foot," I said. "Will you go for help?" He could do that, at any rate, while I stayed with Penuel. "We need the pony also, to carry her to the house."

While I spoke he had moved between me and Penuel, so that I stood on the outside. "You go," he said, using the slow telling syllables of his rare speech. I began to protest. "Help us, please," I begged. "My cousin's ankle is very painful."

"I will cure it. You go, fetch help." He thrust me beyond the door. Before I could recover myself, or protest further, I saw him go to the pallet and lean over Penuel. The hut smelled of herbs and rain. Saginaw lifted Penuel's skirt and drew down her stocking, taking off the garter. She did not cry out. Presently he stooped to the grate and took ashes and began to rub them on the foot, using gentle circular strokes. Penuel accepted everything passively; I thought she must have fainted. Suddenly Saginaw turned and saw me, still watching from the door. "I tell you, go," he said angrily, and flung my cloak at me. "Go to house, fetch pony. I stay here," and then

he strode to the door and, shoving me outside, shot down the
staple of wood that barred the door within, closing the hut.
Penuel had still said nothing aloud but her lips had formed the
words "Go, sweetheart," and her grey-green eyes stared at me
and beyond me. I shall never forget the look they held as long
as I live.

I stood outside in the drizzling rain, my cloak in my hand;
my instinct was to beat on the door and demand to be
admitted, but there was the pony to be fetched. Meantime I
had left her alone in there, with *him*. . . .

I think that I had gone a little way along the track when it
occurred to me that it was wrong, monstrous, to leave the two
of them there alone. I ran back, and put my ear to the door;
there was no sound. I knocked, but no one answered. By then
with my ear against the rough wood I could hear a faint sound
from within. It was like the panting of a dog.

I still cannot think clearly about the time that followed. It is
invaded by a kind of dreamlike terror, which makes it hard to
remember the order in which events took place. I can still
remember, that first night, running, running breathless
through the rain and what had begun to seem evening rather
than day. I stumbled up the steps of Pless portico and almost
fell into the house, and someone caught and held me. It was
Andrew; I can remember clinging to him and sobbing out that
Penuel was hurt, that she was at the hut, that they must bring
the pony quickly. I said nothing about the rest; it seemed to
me that there was no time.

Andrew was very gentle. He said to me "You are soaked
to the skin; Bethia shall dry your clothes and put you to bed;
yes, yes, have no fear, I will go for Penuel." Then Bethia was
there and fussing over me, and I wanted to cry out that it did
not matter that I had been ill, I was better now, but it was
Penuel, Penuel who needed their help, and quickly. But I was
put to bed with a hot brick to my feet, and hot whisky and

milk to drink, and saw nothing of what happened then except that, wonderfully soon, I heard the pony being led away and saw the swaying light of a lantern on the path going down to the plantings.

They brought her home. I was not asleep, and I leaped from my warm bed and went to the window to look, and saw Penuel lifted down from the saddle and carried into the house. She was like a wax doll, lifeless; for an instant the lantern's light caught her face and there was colour in it, and the eyes glistened strangely. I saw her hurt foot hanging as Andrew bore her in his arms up the steps of the portico. The thought came to me then that she did not love Andrew at all, as I had thought; she was miles and years away from him in space and time; she was nobody I knew, nobody at all, and something had happened to change her. We were all of us puppets, pulled by strings: and at this thought I began to weep.

Next day Penuel did not show herself. The day following, a coach was brought to convey her back to town. I saw her go, but I had a slight fever and was not supposed to leave my bed. She sent a farewell to me but did not come to my room, as her foot would not allow her to climb the stairs. I saw her limp to the carriage on Andrew's arm; her hat hid her face.

Within a week she was back. It was then that I knew that the thing which was happening was so monstrous that there were no words to describe it, the thing that had changed Penuel. Her face was still radiant with colour, like a blown rose; she still had the waxy look and the glistening eyes of a doll, and she had no more will than a doll would have against the thing that devoured her. Sometimes when she did not know I was watching she would hold her breasts in her hands, and moan softly; and there was the night when, because the hasp of my window-shutter had broken loose and flapped in the wind, I rose to mend it, having had a disturbed sleep till dawn. Then I caught sight of Penuel, in the garden below, gliding past the pruned trees like a phantom, walking as if her foot no longer hurt, as if she had no weight at all and would hardly leave her footprints on the dewy grass. She had been to the hut; I could tell it. Then there was the other time, the day after Andrew rode off south; the time I walked Pleasance through the woods lest he catch his hoof, for the ground was uneven after the digging of last year. The earth was soft and we made no sound. I came on them together; they lay on the earth, the man's dark profile triumphant, aware as a hawk's, and he must have known I was there but cared nothing. Penuel did not know. She lay below him, the fair head sullied by contact with the earth, lips parted and moist, eyes closed. I stood there motionless, staring, watching the Indian's active buttocks grow taut and still: and presently heard a sound that, though it was the answer to all that had happened, I did not understand; the cry, from deep down, of ecstasy of a woman fulfilled. I had never before known of it and I would never forget it again. They say we are animals. Perhaps it is true.

I turned the pony's head and returned by the way I had come, in silence. This unchildlike state was aided by my trembling certainty. Penuel the paragon, the botanist, acquainted with genteel Edinburgh, modest, mannerly and cold, had warmed her fires now to a perverse enchantment I could not begin to fathom, for it denied almost everything I had ever loved in her. I faced the situation as it was for myself, knowing I must do so. I knew Penuel went out nightly and, now Andrew had ridden off, also by day to visit the Indian, and lie with him.

# *Ten*

I was glad to return to school alone in Penuel's hired coach; she had chosen to stay on at Pless while the weather was fine. I did not feel that I wanted to be close to her yet on a long journey; the kiss on parting had been bad enough and I had thought of her cool mouth growing soft and moist under Saginaw's. As the landscape changed and the hills grew round and low-lying as they are in the east, I tried to put the whole matter of the Indian out of my mind. It was like a nightmare, I thought, no more. I must not think of it; and instead I tried to fix my mind on the things which were to happen this term, the prim walks to St. Giles's on Sundays in our red cloaks, the sketching out of doors to which Miss Crindle, who had some skill with a pencil, would take some of us on good days, and the assembly which would finish the school year and for which we were all assiduously practising our dancing. The older girls might each invite one young gentleman of approved character, but I was not yet old enough to do so, despite the fact that I was married. I reflected on my peculiar state and, to pass the time, on the husband I still scarcely knew. Thinking of him brought me back again to Penuel, so I switched my thoughts instead to the nearest person I could find; Thornton, whom I had hardly glimpsed except once in church and who had so far never visited me, which was not singular. No doubt he would tell Penuel and myself that his duties kept him from visiting; but I suspected that he led a very gay life in the town, and would have small time for his sister and his cousin. Even this thought made me mournful, and I found myself in a very abject state as the coach drew near Edinburgh.

After the first few days at school, the pleasure of seeing Mary again—"You haven't missed much, Primrose, it has rained all the time and we have hardly been out. How you've grown! And you are thinner,"—and such others as I had exchanges with, I found I was no longer sad. On the contrary, a devil of resentment seemed to have entered into me and I did everything I could to make poor old Crindle's life a misery, and soon had the rest copying me. For a group of docile young girls to turn into she-demons is not permissible for long, and soon I had a summons from Mrs. McLehose to answer for my behaviour, for I was known to be the ringleader. She received me coldly and I did not dare fix my eyes even on the bow in her bonnet. By her side on the table was a parcel and a letter, and reading it upside down while she talked I saw that it was addressed to me. Anger rose in me; how dare she keep my letters?

"—and we had hopes that ye might leave here a passably accomplished young leedy, but now ye are a hoyden, and what is worse, make the others so. Unless there is an improvement I fear I must inform Mr. Fairquharson of your bad influence." I have not attempted to mimic her style all through; the mixture of gentility and underlying plain Scots was comical enough to take away all the effect of her lecture. Why could she not speak as came naturally to her? I fixed my eyes on my letter, wondering from whom it had come. Finally the offended lady mentioned it, stretching out her hand, which was none too clean.

"I had considered withholding this, and the peckage, which are from your husband. However on reflection, it is as well to let ye have them; remember what I have said, and try to improve in future." I took the letter; it had been already opened. Rage overflowed in me. "What right have you to read my letters?" I blurted out; whatever Andrew had to say, it was spoilt for me by reason of this beldame's having seen it first. Tears blurred my vision and I could not read what he had written; the hand was small and neat, the whole taking up only a single sheet of paper. Mrs. McLehose bridled audibly, her stays creaking.

"A fine thing if we were to let every young miss receive letters from no matter whom! You will submit your reply to me, if you please. These are the rules of the establishment."

"Then I will not reply."

"You are an impudent minx. Take your letter to the window, if you please, and read it, and then go back to your proper concerns." I went to the window, anger still choking me; but it would be best to see what Andrew had to say. He wrote from London.

*My Dear Wife*, the letter read (fancy old McLehose having the impudence, herself, to open the seal and ...) *This as you will see finds me still in the Capital, and there has been a deal to do with the Cargo of Skins, two of the Best of which I have had made into a Muff, which goes by this same Post as I never made you any Wedding Gift. I hope that it will keep your Hands warm in Church. I hope also that you are Diligent and are learning all things New that you may.* (No, I am an impudent minx; madam here says so.)

*I was indeed Sorry when you had the Measles, but better now than later. I myself will not be back at Pless for some time, and may even be away all Summer. I may even have to take Ship to see to affairs of my Company in Montreal, for it is of little use leaving Everything to Other Folk. When I return, we may perhaps meet soon.*

*Till then, I am your devoted husband and Friend,*

*Andrew Farquharson.*

Later I stroked the silky fur of the muff, and basked in the envy of the other girls. I would not let them put their sweaty hands inside, except for Mary who kept herself clean.

The result of all this was that I did not answer Andrew's letter, or thank him for the muff. I told myself that it was because I refused to have my letters supervised by anyone; but within my mind I knew it was for another reason. If Andrew had not guessed the state of affairs at Pless, if his love for Penuel had not made him sensitive to the change in her, then he must be stupid.

There was another thing; I was not going to mend my ways. I had not asked my husband to send me to school, nor did I like it here, though it was better for the moment than Pless, over which there always fell, these days, the shadow of Saginaw.

# Eleven

WHEN MRS. MCLEHOSE sent for me soon after that I thought it was for a fresh homily about my bad manners, but she kissed me, a sure sign of calamity. The news was sad in its way, though it did not affect me and I made little pretence that it did. My father was dead. He had been found seated as usual beside his unfinished game of chess, which now would never be completed. "Poor orphaned child," said McLehose, and stroked and caressed me, which I disliked. I drew away as soon as I could from her smells of age and stale verbena. "Ye shed no tears, Mrs. Fairquharson," she said then, as if I had committed some breach of etiquette; no doubt it was one.

"We never cared for one another," I answered evenly.

"How can ye say such things? I perceive a lack of all proper feeling in ye."

"I am telling the truth; is that a fault?" And, I was thinking, he deceived my mother abominably and never in his life took thought for me, or anyone except himself. No doubt I had inherited his selfishness. The bow on the headmistress's bonnet was undergoing its customary emotional tremors. The thought occurred to me that it must have shaken notably at the death of Mr. McLehose. Who had he been? None of us had ever heard of him; perhaps he was an invention. This notion enabled me to look the good lady in the eye as she went on with her task of trying to refine my feelings.

"At your age, child, it is unbecoming to be so haird."

"Why is it unbecoming, if so I am?"

"It should be disguised, for no one loves a flint-hairted young woman. Decorum must be obsairved; that is of the first importance. Your cousin Leedy Munro writes that she will return to town shortly, when you may wait on her. It has been decided that ye are not to travel home for the obsequies."

Indeed, I thought, by this time those would already be over and father's pallid remains transferred to the Tebb vault, beside my mother. I wondered who had decided that I was not to be present. I confronted McLehose with the question. She bridled like a pigeon settling down into its roost.

"Your husband decided it, for your good, I doubt not." The bonnet was still; no doubt it would have been more proper for me to be sent down to Pless in black bombazine, weeping into a black-bordered handkerchief. However the second part of the news disturbed me, and made me tremble. I did not want to see Penuel when she returned to town. McLehose was watching me with a beady eye and I think that she had convinced herself that at last I was showing proper sentiments. She asked if I would like to go and lie down on my bed, and I shook my head. The fleas could keep their own company.

"Will Lady Munro be here soon?" I asked steadily.

"After the funeral. It is she who writes."

So Penuel had written, but not to me; and Andrew, who must have returned, had decreed that I was not to come to Pless. Perhaps, I thought, he was angry because I had not thanked him for the muff. Perhaps also—this made my heart stop—he had after all guessed something of the affair between Penuel and Saginaw. How would he act now towards his blood-brother?

I left the headmistress's room in subdued fashion, which needed no pretence for I was afraid. The rest of that day I spent alone, as far as one could do so in such a place. My behaviour was put down to the fact of my father's death, and they were lenient with me.

When word came that Penuel had returned I pretended to be ill. I lay in bed and moaned that my courses were hurting me (in fact they have never caused me more than ordinary inconvenience). Some time later poor old Crindle came to see me, a sure sign of real emergency; McLehose was for show only. My cousin was herself ill, I was told; she had asked particularly that I should go to her, and had sent a carriage.

I rose and dressed quickly in order not to keep the carriage waiting in the narrow street. I knew that Penuel's illness, at any rate, must be genuine; she was less of a liar than I was. Much of my unwillingness to see her had left me by the time the carriage had jolted down the street. I jumped out past the footman's hand and hurried into the house.

To my disappointment, Penuel had company; she was not even in bed, but seated on her sofa with her face against the light. She kissed me, I thought, absently. A middle-aged exquisite had called, and some time was spent in converse with him; he seemed likely never to leave, and had stayed for half an hour when Penuel, rising, excused us, to my surprise, saying that we had to go out. During the time the departing visitor made his compliments I took leisure to look at Penuel with the daylight on her. Certainly she did not look well. She had used her rouge, which she seldom did, and I could see that it hid a pallor which was not like her pretty colour: her mouth looked bruised and her eyes shadowed. I clenched my fingers hard into my fists. It had all come back, the sight of her with Saginaw; when we were alone I knew I must ask her about herself.

There was no need. Penuel saw the visitor out and I heard

her tell the servant to say that she was not at home to other callers. Then she came back into the room where I was and flung up her hands to her face and burst into passionate weeping.

I sat still. I knew that no ordinary comfort would ease her. The fair hair gleamed wanly in the daylight from the street. Penuel turned away at last and, biting her lips, sat down. I had not spoken. She looked at me strangely.

"You know it all, Primrose, do you not? A child like you. I was mad; mad. Perhaps one day you will understand."

She paused, and I still kept silent. It would be useless to say any of the things that came into my head. My silence calmed her, I believe, because she went on as though it had all of it happened to someone else. "He shut me out," she said, "at the last. I went to him at the hut—you remember—and it was barred from the inside and I could hear them laugh, the two of them."

"Andrew?" I said. She shook her head, frowning a little. "How could it have been? He knew nothing, I swear. Andrew has nothing in his mind but his trees, and they make him blind. No, it was a woman inside with—him. I always knew he had other women. But to bar the door against me, and laugh with her. . . . And afterwards he said he had had enough of me. He said that to me, to me . . . and there is another thing. I am with child. I am like the farm-women he got with brown babies; oh, yes, I remember you told me what Bethia said. I cannot let it be born. That was why I sent for you; I would have no one else know of this, but I cannot go alone to—to the place I must."

She looked at me and seeing me stare in lack of comprehension came over and took my face in her hands. I had wondered how I could ever let her touch me again. Now it did not matter, provided it brought her comfort, poor Penuel.

"You are a child still," she said. "I should not ask it of you.

But I care for no other. It—it may mean my death to have this done. I know it, but I must go, today. Afterwards we will come back here. It is almost time; I thought that man would never go." She turned away abruptly and stared out of the window as if it interested her what went on in the street. For the time it took a cart to trundle past I still did not speak, and then I heard myself say, through stiff lips, "I will come with you." I still was not sure what she meant or where she was going. I was a child, as she had said. But if Penuel needed me I would come with her. It occurred to me that Thornton, as her brother, might help. I mentioned his name and she flung round.

"Thornton? He must not be told on any account. You must never mention it to a living soul; promise me, swear. Afterwards it must be as if nothing had ever gone amiss. I shall not return to Pless. In any case—" she gave a little wry smile— "since Uncle James died I cannot stay on there, it would not be proper. Your Andrew is a great man for the proprieties, Primrose. He spent the last few nights before the funeral at an inn."

I thought of Saginaw and how fortunate it was that she had not been found with him. Then I thought of Pless and how neither of us might see it again, myself for years, Penuel perhaps never. I began to cry and said "Penuel, you are not going to die. You must not—you must not—" I do not know what more I said. She came over and, as if I were the one who needed comfort, held me in her arms and caressed me, till it was time to go. If anyone saw us with tear-stained faces it would be taken that we grieved for my father, whom nobody in this world grieved over at all.

"No doctor will deal with such things," Penuel had told me before we left in the hired carriage, entering it a few doors down the street. "There is a—a woman who lives behind the Canongate who is adept at them. If you will, stay in the carriage. I can endure it if I know you are close by."

"I will come with you," I said again.

She had entered the carriage veiled, wearing an unfamiliar cloak. Even outside her own house they might not have known her. After the carriage drove off and turned from the main way I was astonished at the swift change from the Edinburgh we knew, the place of genteel calls and lawyers and polite tea-drinkings. The very buildings seemed to have grown old and wicked with age, their dark arcades holding unsavoury things, their upper parts leaning crazily half across the street. At one such place we stopped, and Penuel told the driver to wait. When we got out she took my arm and I could feel that she was trembling. "This is not the house," she whispered, "it's down the next pend." Even the driver, evidently, was not to know where we went. I wondered if he had come on many such drives. I followed Penuel down the narrow outside passage where two could hardly walk abreast; above, rags of washing hung, roped high between one leaning house and the other.

"This is the place," said Penuel in a low voice at last, and I could smell the stuffy air of the close-entry, fouled with excrement. The turret at the Lawnmarket, which I had thought unsavoury, seemed a world away. Had I ever thought of Raisin Pudding as unclean? She would never have shown herself here.

We ascended the stairs and knocked on a door. It was already partly open and I sensed that the woman who opened it had known of our coming since we first turned into the close. I will not describe her, except that she had a red face, a grimy cap, and hands that were not clean. I dared not look at her hands a second time. How could Penuel endure the touch of them? Yet she even endured the woman's familiar speech. It was in such broad Scots that I could not follow it, but the creature spoke as to an equal. Penuel turned to me, speaking through her veil.

"She says that you cannot come in, that you must wait outside here. At the least I know that you are near. It will not be long." She was no longer trembling; she seemed now to be fashioned of cold metal, like a sword.

"I will be here," I said. I had forgotten the coachman and my earlier fear that he might not after all wait in such a place. All my thoughts now were for Penuel. For almost the first time in my life, I prayed. I had watched her follow the woman into a room where the window was too small and encrusted with dirt to admit much daylight. All I could see was a bed with a filthy coverlet and pillows. The door closed. I stood with my back against the close-wall, suddenly dizzy. The woman would hurt Penuel, I knew. Would she also rob her while she lay helpless? I should have taken her purse for her, perhaps her ring. At that moment I felt like an old, knowing woman. I became aware that the foul smell in the narrow passage came partly from an open privy, which flowed down the inner wall into the pend below. It came near to overpowering me. I shut my eyes.

There was nothing but silence from the house. Presently the door opened and the woman came out. She did not look at me. She was carrying a shallow dish in her hands. I had caught sight of the inner room and the bed, with Penuel lying on it white as paper. I tried to go to her, and then the woman laid a hand on me.

"Nae need for a bairn to gang in yonder. She'll come to ye sune."

She went towards the privy, and emptied the contents of the dish into it. I had seen them. There was blood, and, floating in it, a tiny thing, a beginning of a life, with grotesque bowed head and fingerless growths for limbs. I cannot recall any feeling, even horror, then. That was to come later, and remain hidden at the back of my brain, like poison, for many years. I began to tremble, it is true, after the woman returned inside. I stared on at the closed door, feeling sick.

In a short time—it was shockingly soon—Penuel herself was let out, reeling and faint. She had forgotten to replace her veil. I gave her my arm and gently drew the veil over her face and together, slowly, my arm supporting her, we went down the twisting stairs. The fear began to nag at me again that the coachman would have gone, and how then was I to get Penuel home?

But he had waited. We entered the coach and he drove off. I can recall the crowd of barefoot children who had clustered round, scattering as we drove away, jeering because we had thrown no pennies. A stone followed the coach and I heard it hit the place between the wheels. The coachman cursed and spat. I thought suddenly "He cannot know who we are or he would not have acted so," and this comforted me. Penuel lay back against the cushions with her eyes closed. We had said nothing to each other, but she kept hold of my hand. The journey was jolting and uncomfortable and I was afraid for her.

"Tell him to stop where we got in," she said at last faintly, as our street was reached. I replied with sudden fierceness "No, he'll take you home. You will not walk as far," and when the time came I tapped on the glass and made the man drive on a little, and Penuel gave me her purse and I paid him, and he helped me to take her up the steps to her own door. I had concocted a tale to say she had been taken ill in the street. When the servant opened the door I told it, and said Lady Munro must go at once to bed; no one questioned it but when the servant asked if a physician should be fetched, Penuel said faintly "No. I shall be well presently."

The servants took her from me and I saw her borne away, and suddenly felt my own knees grow weak and went to the sofa and sat down. I mustn't be sick, I told myself. I must keep up the tale I'd told. I swallowed, took deep breaths and felt better. I turned, as Penuel had done earlier, to look out of the window at the familiar street. That other must be forgotten, and what had been done and what I had seen. I must speak of it to no one, not even to Penuel when she should be well again. She *must* grow better, in her body and in her mind. It did not signify if she and I never saw Pless again.

I stayed at Penuel's house that night. Next day I did not see
her as she stayed in bed, and the servant came to ask me if she
should send after all for a physician and I said "No," as
Penuel had done.

Next day after that she sent for me. I went, and was shocked
by her looks; she was flushed and hectic with fever, her lips
bitten and dry. Her eyes wandered restlessly and her thin
hands plucked at the covers, and I went and knelt by her and
said "It is Primrose, dearest. You are better, are you not?"
But I knew that she was worse, not better. I took a cloth and
dipped it in the closet-jug and tried to moisten her lips, and
wondered again if I should send for a physician in spite of all
that had been done. She was beginning to talk brokenly,
most of it rambling nonsense, and I said "Rest, Penuel. You
must get well," and then I think she felt my tears on her hand,
because she whispered "Talk to me of wild flowers. You know
nearly as many as I do," and smiled, and I said over their names,
the flowers and plants she had loved to find and press into a
book and label clearly; fennel, chervil, dog-rose, campion, fool's
parsley, St. John's wort, honeysuckle, bedstraw, ragged robin,
Queen's lace, clary, eyebright, buttercup, marsh marigold, the
rest. She fell quiet and listened, while I hunted in my mind for
more and more flowers to remember; then suddenly Penuel
drew up her knees with a little sigh and when I looked at her
I could see that she heard nothing any more.

# Twelve

PENUEL'S FUNERAL might have been that of someone I did not know. While the long-faced executors were going about their business in the house I had lain face down on my bed, howling like a dog. When I was put into the mourning-dress bought earlier for father's death I had no more tears to shed. Swollen-eyed, I watched them all come, all the genteel of town, and view the coffin in which Penuel's body lay, fair as a wax image and as lifeless. Later there was a hearse drawn by matched black horses wearing sable plumes, fringes, all the trappings of the prosperous dead. Penuel was to be buried beside her old husband, whom she had not loved and would never have wanted to lie beside, in life or death. I wanted to cry out the truth of the matter, but to whom? I was already in disfavour, for everyone was whispering that I should have fetched a physician to Penuel when she was dying of, they said, a sudden fever. I can remember Thornton, his face already growing lax about the jaw with easy living, blaming me bitterly in front of them all. "You are no longer a child; anyone else would have had enough sense to fetch a doctor to her!" No, Thornton, I was no longer a child by then, but you would never know why.

So there it was; Lady Munro, widow of a judge, was to share a cold bed with his bones. Even Mrs. McLehose, impressed by all the consequence, hastened to show herself at the funeral service, dressed in a fearsome new bonnet with weepers. Solemn lawyers in their black clothes came, all in carriages, which would wind uphill behind the handsome coffin with its polished shining handles. It was all of it a sham, and Penuel would have shunned it.

My husband came to the funeral, having ridden by himself up from Pless. When we first met I stared at him, thinking beyond my grief to notice how presentable he had made himself. His sandy hair was carefully combed and pomaded, as it had been for our wedding, and tied with a black riband. His mourning-linen and his hands, roughened with hard work as they were, were scrupulously clean. Whatever Andrew was feeling did not show on his face; this was blunt and set, as usual. He had come and stood by me while Thornton made his outburst, and had sent the latter away.

We were alone for a moment and I said in a low voice, so that no one else should hear, "You loved Penuel, I know, from the start."

He smiled gently. "It was impossible not to love her," he said. "You yourself did so."

"Yet I have just been told I killed her."

"Do not heed that fool," was all he would say. He looked to the ground. "It is perhaps fitting that she should die young, and still lovely. Can one picture her as old?"

I wanted to shout "Fool yourself, your blood-brother got her with child lying in the woods, and she died of letting some filthy woman in the back slums tear it from her and then turn her out of the house," but I did not. Whatever else happened, Andrew must never know the truth of Penuel's death. I think it was that resolve that ended my childhood, for I kept silence. I said instead, flatly, "I never thanked you for the muff."

He lifted his head, and the strained look in his eyes lightened for instants, as though he reminded himself he was indulging the child who was his wife. I said "Old McLehose—" I could see her, seated preening herself among the visiting black-clad matrons— "would have supervised the letter and made me rewrite it as she chose. So I didn't send one."

He said to me, still in the same indulgent voice, "But you are not unhappy at school, Primrose? When this is over, you will return to your friends and your studies. You are there, as you know, to learn." His smile stayed fixed, and I reflected that after all he was paying out silver to old McLehose and would expect to receive value for money in the shape of a well-turned-out wife, docile and knowledgeable, at the end. I put my nose in the air and said that as a rule I was neither happy nor unhappy. "When," I said, "can I come home to Pless?" For with Penuel's death the dread of the Indian had vanished: he would not, I swore, harm me. Besides, lacking Penuel, there was nowhere else I could certainly go for holidays. I stared sullenly at the matrons munching biscuits and sipping ratafia. They thought of death as an occasion for nibbles and gossip, and had no feelings; or so I decided.

Andrew meantime had begun to reply in his thoughtful way. "Pless is no fit place yet for a young lady," he told me.

"I was never a lady till you tried to turn me into one."

"Do not speak so loudly," he said, "they are watching you, and it is improper. At Pless we live and eat roughly, more so than in the days of your father, and are out all day at work on the trees. It is almost time to select the queen."

"It seems that there has been nothing but talk of trees since we two met," I said ungratefully.

"Maybe," he said with unvarying calm. "But they grow well, I believe, and am thankful for it."

He bowed, and moved away from me to talk to some of the mourners. In the evening I shared a carriage with Mrs. McLehose to return to school. I cannot recall whether or not I said goodbye to my husband.

## Thirteen

PENUEL'S DEATH, and its reason, were to have disastrous consequences for me within the year. Although I have said that in my mind I was no longer a child, I was as yet in my body neither child nor woman. The remembrance of what had happened to Penuel is mingled in my mind with the change from my childhood's flat thin-limbed contours to another; to a shape with pert little breasts, a slender waist, plump arms and legs and a skin as smooth as a petal. My dark hair was still short, and curled naturally. Since then I have been told that I resembled a painting by Greuze of that youthful shepherdess with outward innocence, but showing one breast, as though her tunic had slipped by accident. Such was I, and it may be magined that the school in the Lawnmarket was not the place for me.

I had become very naughty, and impatient of restraint. I was often sent for to McLehose, whose prosing did me no good as I only mocked at it. I did everything that could be thought of to upset discipline and the smooth running of the school; I was the despair of both dancing-master and drawing-master, and made daubs of my paintings; moreover, I had upset the poor old aristocrat's slop-pail which he carried so tenderly downstairs each day, causing him to stumble and spill it. The unsavoury contents cascaded down the spiral stairs, which had to be cleansed with much water and made the school giggle for days. I am sure that only my married status preserved me from a whipping; there was no end to the tribulations of Mrs. McLehose and Miss Crindle. The former sent for me once and, face set like a fury's, described my sinful ways and announced that she would pray that they be improved: only the Power from on high could save me. But even this source of influence was interfered with, for I flirted openly by now in church. When this was observed by McLehose she said that anyone who acted in such a way was reserved for a bad end, and she washed her hands of me. "And if I have one more complaint concairning yer conduct, Mrs. Fairquharson, I shall be obleeged to send for your goodman to take ye away."

I did not care whether I stayed or went, and continued as before. Church was certainly less dull for my occupation, in which Mary joined me. By now I had seen Thornton lounge into the back pews several times, and such of his fellow-officers as were with him were destined bait for my hook. I never listened to the sermon, about which we were afterwards set to write a prose précis; the time had been spent in backward glances from under my bonnet. Mary likewise found it a delicious game; she was more steadfast than I, for her attention was fixed on one young officer only, and we had discovered by some means that his name was Alan Sutherland. As for me, any man in uniform would do, provided he was reasonably tall.

All in all, when McLehose sent for me again I thought it must be to receive my marching-orders. I tidied my hair and went to her, my heart sinking into my slippers; most of my wicked behaviour was mere boasting, and I was no less of a coward than I had ever been. Mrs. McLehose did not at once survey me. She was reading a letter she held, adjusting her steel-rimmed spectacles that she might see it better. Her mouth hardened to a tight line over its china contents.

"I hairdly know whether or not it is wise to grant ye this liberty, Mrs. Fairquharson, as ye have taken so many," she began. "Neither you nor Miss Cantlie, who is your follower in everything, have my approval." But we both paid for extra lessons, I thought. "A letter from your cousin, Lieutenant Milhall—" I downed my surprise; what could Thornton be at suddenly to recall my existence?— "says that he has your husband's permission to take you and Miss Cantlie out for some diversion this coming Saturday. I am, as I say, not cairtain whether—"

I cut in eagerly with the reminder that Thornton was Lady Munro's brother. "Any connection of *hers* must be beyond reproach, to be sure," the headmistress acknowledged, with a sigh and a hand to her heart. Finally she stated that she was prepared to allow Mary and myself to accept the invitation, provided Miss Crindle went with us as chaperon. I disguised my dismay.

I was intrigued. I knew perfectly well that Thornton would never have troubled to find out Andrew's opinion, any more than he had troubled with me all the time I had been at school, until now. I had the satisfaction of knowing that McLehose would accept for us, and would perhaps mention Miss Crindle, and I pictured Thornton's face on receiving that news. For the rest of the week Mary and I quenched our excitement, lest at the last moment permission would be withdrawn as a punishment.

"Where can we go with old Crindle by us?" grumbled Mary one night in bed. The rest were sleeping, or else pretending to; their backs were turned. I said I did not know, except that we might push Crindle in the Nor' Loch. Then Mary wondered if Alan Sutherland would be there.

"I am sure he has noticed me, Primrose. He always occupies the place behind where I sit, as near as he can, and he watches me all through the sermon."

"Well, we must wait and see," I said, and yawned, for I was sleepy.

Lieutenant Sutherland at least did not show himself in McLehose's parlour, but Thornton did; he had enough impudence for anything. Mary and I, suitably clad in our second best—I was by now again in half mourning, and wore lilac, with a fichu which showed off my new bosom while affecting to conceal it, and Mary was in yellow, and our summer hats were of straw—were led into the chamber, and Thornton rose and made his best bow. I know he had been using his prodigious charm to persuade old McLehose that he was a virtuous and suitable young man to be escort to two of her young ladies and one old one. We set off, accompanied by Crindle, down the stairs, with Thornton's high-polished military boots clattering behind us. He was resplendent in powder and his red coat with gold braid, and I briefly remembered borrowing his ragged breeches in our old days at Pless.

At the foot of the stairs poor Crindle bridled coyly. "Ye will not force two tender young things, and an auld body, to walk too fast and too far?" Thornton bowed again and assured her he had a carriage waiting, and gave her his arm most gallantly. "It is standing some little way down the street, for it is too narrow to turn here without going up again towards the Castle." He spoke as if the carriage were his personal means of conveyance and the Castle his private residence. I had begun to giggle and I knew Mary was in the same state.

I had known there would be some trick, and what this was became evident the moment Mary's Lieutenant Sutherland, smiling all over his face, was met by us where he stood at the hired carriage, ready to open the door. He leapt to attention, bowed to Miss Crindle and watched Thornton hand her in with the greatest of ceremony. I felt Thornton squeeze my elbow and, no doubt, the lieutenant squeezed Mary's. However it might be, the coach door was slammed shut and the driver, who had meantime been gazing at St. Giles's steeple, flourished his whip and started off at a cracking pace, sending the folk scattering nearby to avoid being run over. I saw poor Crindle holding up her mittened hands to heaven and the O of dismay her mouth made, and that is the last we saw of her. My first thought was of the lecture she would receive from her sister on return. "Never fear, she will still be a virgin when they get to Holyrood," muttered Thornton. He took my elbow in a firm grasp and we almost ran down a side-street. Mary's giggles had become uncontrollable and soon we were all four in a like state. "You'll have us put into the black book with your tricks," I spluttered, "and they will lock us up on bread and water."

"Then let us make up for it by going to an eating-house and downing steak pie and ale. Come quickly, before the old virgin pays the man more than I did to land her back again."

We were still hurrying, too much so for decorum on the part of McLehose's young ladies; I had my cousin's arm and Mary had Sutherland's, but as far as I could hear they only giggled still, and exchanged no words. Sutherland himself I had summed up at once, being less blinded by the dart of love than Mary, who was usually so sharp; he was no more than a great schoolboy all grins and blushes; I had no doubt whatever that the trick itself was Thornton's. "I hope," I said to him when I could gain breath, "that this inventiveness of yours will promote you to captain."

I batted my eyelashes at him as I did now to all men, and was thrown into some confusion when I saw the way he, who had known me all my days, was looking at me, with his eyes narrowed and the expression of a man who assesses the points of a filly for sale. I resolved to show him, if so, that I was not to be bought. But he had begun to talk to me, in a low voice like a lover's.

"You are grown a beauty, Primrose; who'd have thought

it after the little wildcat you used to be, in my borrowed breeches and with never a comb through your hair? I've watched you often, flirting away in church; half the men are mad for you; I never was close enough till now to see the difference since my sister's burying."

"You spoke unkindly enough to me then."

"And regret it now. Not a spot or blemish on you; teeth sound and a fine front deck, or 'twill be in a year or so, when Andrew has made a woman of you, rot him."

"Do you compare me to a horse or a battleship?" My heart was pounding, for he had touched on a subject I did not wish to think of, and I did not even remind or tease him about how we might once have married one another, but had not. Looking at Thornton now I was glad; he had a rakish air despite his smart uniform, and the wavering jawline I had noted at Penuel's funeral threatened soon to run to fat. He was a young man who, I doubted not, indulged himself in every way. Well, he should not do so with me; I resolved to keep a rein on my own behaviour, and if possible on Mary's.

We were walking now at greater leisure through the vennels, swept by the winds and cleaner than the dreadful place I had been in with Penuel. The houses still leaned towards one another and there was washing hung out, as always. I chattered of everyday things to keep my thoughts from that other day, and also from the punishment we might well expect when we returned to school. But I was not going to spoil Mary's pleasure, or my own; it was pleasant to take a turn about the streets on a young man's arm, so different from walking in double file to church with McLehose at one end and Crindle at the other. I wondered briefly what had befallen poor Crindle and if she had the return fare, or had been forced to walk back all the way from Holyrood, where Thornton had paid the driver to set her down. Certainly we had used her churlishly, but for the moment I did not care. The present was to enjoy, and devil take the future.

Thornton was laughing at something I had said and then, without any warning, ushered me in, with a caution to mind my head, past the low door of an eating-house. The place inside was thick with tobacco-smoke, through which could dimly be seen the shining of lanthorns. It might have been night instead of day. Gradually I made out the benches and tables at which ordinary folk, mostly men, were seated drinking ale, and there was a smell of good cooking beyond the reek of the clay pipes. We all sat down and Thornton ordered meat pies and ale. "They make good pies here," he told us. Mary looked, I thought, a trifle pale, and the smoke made her cough. But she smiled valiantly and tried to make eye-play with her lieutenant, who had not as yet been heard to utter a single sound. I tried to rally him.

"Must we drink ale? It is not a lady's drink, as you will know. Have they no other?" But Mary's young man only blinked and stammered and looked at Thornton, who shook his head in a knowledgeable manner.

"The only other thing they serve here is whisky," he said, "and we had best not send you back to school smelling of that."

Mary shrieked with laughter and we settled down to enjoy ourselves. The pies were brought and were good, steaming hot and full of meat, far better than anything we had at McLehose's. As for the ale, I took a sip and thought it bitter. But after the salty meat it was needed to quench our thirst, and by the end my head was swimming and I knew Mary's was likewise.

"Now you are a rose, not a primrose," said Thornton, referring to the bright colour I knew had crept up in my cheeks. He ordered more ale and tried to press me to it, but I refused, and Mary did so also. He and Sutherland drank on and presently the latter began to talk, telling one or two stories which were so improper I was surprised he knew them. But I laughed loudly and Mary joined in, and when we left the ale-house to take a turn about the town (Crindle should be home again by this time) I swear both our hats were askew. The cold air struck me in the face and sobered me. We spent a merry afternoon among the booths and in the bookshops behind the colonnades, and I saw one place where they sold heart-shaped silver brooches like the one I had given Penuel. I shut my eyes for an instant. She wore it now in her grave.

The reception awaiting us on our return was even worse than I had expected. Thornton, to do him justice, came up with us, and tried to delude McLehose with a story that the horse had run away before we could all of us get inside the coach, but not surprisingly the headmistress did not believe him. He was dismissed with the utmost coldness, and a promise that a letter complaining of his ill conduct would be sent to his colonel. This struck him on the raw; the last I saw of him was a jaw-dropped face, with most of its confidence gone.

We had had our jaunt, and now must pay for it. Nothing would induce McLehose to believe that I had not known about everything beforehand. For two young ladies of *the school* to have lent themselves to such behaviour was beyond everything; it would perhaps not have been quite as bad, I deduced, in young ladies from anywhere else. It was useless to say that all we had done was to eat steak pies (I missed out the ale) and gaze at the shops. I heard afterwards, for I was not permitted to see her again, of Mary's punishment; to her great indignation she was birched, and was told that if she as much as turned her head once in church in the future it would happen again. As for me, my married state ruled out such a punishment, so a worse fate awaited me. I was to be expelled. Having been told that my husband had been sent for to remove me, I was put and kept in a locked room and permitted to see no one except the servant who brought me my meals, and she had strict orders not to speak to me. I spent the time, therefore, scratching patterns on the whitewashed wall with my bodice-pin, as prisoners have done throughout history. The food they brought me was not bread and water, granted; it was the ordinary school fare, of which I persuaded myself I would be glad to be quit.

I wondered about Andrew and whether or not he would be very angry. Perhaps he would birch me as they had done to Mary. The worst thing for him, I knew, would be that he must be dragged away from his beloved trees to come and fetch me. Perhaps what he would use on me would not be a birch bough, but one of Polyphemus fir. I diverted myself with this possibility as the hours and days passed, for he did not immediately come to my release.

At last word came to my penitential cell that Andrew was waiting. He had taken his own time to come, I thought, for by now I was as angry with him as he would probably be with me. Half of me was glad to see him and the other half uncertain of what he would do. McLehose, her dire speeches evidently exhausted, had left him alone to receive me. On my entrance he rose from where he had been sitting, his plain tricorne hat dangling between his hands, and made me a curt bow. I bobbed a curtsy. After that it did not seem as if we had many words to exchange. I watched Andrew's expression carefully. As usual, it did not tell the casual beholder anything. Dogged, stubborn, blunt of feature, controlled, all these words might have applied—but presently there came over it a changed look, and I remembered, as if it were a card to play in my hand, that Thornton had told me I was become a beauty. I used this knowledge shamelessly upon Andrew from the second or third moment of our meeting. I spared him nothing; whatever he had been going to say was banished from his recollection, and he opened and shut his mouth like a fish. Presently he said, in a gasping voice, as if the fish were hooked and laid upon the bank, "I have been closeted with your headmistress."

I burst out laughing. I could not help it; the picture of Andrew closeted with McLehose, her chin, teeth, her trembling bow and bosom, was too much. Perhaps he had found it so also. His set features relaxed a trifle and he said, trying not to smile or laugh, "Primrose, I should be very displeased with you."

"But you are not?" Here indeed was a feather in my cap; and it was prowess indeed to flirt successfully with one's own husband. I used my eyelashes to their full effect, but this time Andrew did not respond. He was looking grave again and said "From what I have been able to learn, the fault was less yours than Thornton's. He is most irresponsible. If I say no more about this to you, it is on condition that you promise never to go anywhere alone with Thornton again."

"May I go out with other young men?"

"Do not be foolish; of course you may not." He was silent and I said at last "Do we then leave soon for home? My gear will be all of it packed and roped, depend on it; they are glad to see the back of me."

"And you are glad likewise, no doubt. But you are not going home."

"Not to Pless?" All the blood left my face, and its whiteness must have touched him, because he came and placed my arm in his, and said "Let us go down to the coach, and I will tell you more. You shall come to Pless soon, I promise you; but not now."

"Why not?" I stamped my foot, a thing one seldom does in fact, but I was angry and hurt. Not to go home! To be sent to another school, a second McLehose, more fleas and dough-pudding and spotty company and four to a bed! How could he condemn me to it? I opened my mouth to speak, but Andrew answered gently. It occurred to me that he was, when all was said, treating me very well.

"Because, as I have told you before, the house is not yet fit for my wife to live in, and because the trees at present take up all my time and I would have none left for you, or for anyone. It has been inconvenient to have come even on this journey at this time of year. Fortunately Saginaw is left in charge, but I must go back without delay."

"You took your time in coming here, at any rate. I thought I would never win free of that room," I muttered. I did not want to speak of Saginaw. Andrew replied, still in a milder tone than I deserved, "That was because I had to ride first to the place where I am taking you now, to make sure you could be accommodated. It is not a school; you may like it better, I believe, than this, and no one will make you play the harpsichord or learn the globes, or any of the other things you would not be diligent at in the Lawnmarket."

"The globes are dull."

"Indeed they are not, if you had travelled them."

"Where are you taking me? Is it to an orphanage? Nothing would surprise me, I declare."

He frowned a little. "Remember your manners, if you have any, and do not speak so to me. I am taking you to stay with two cousins of my mother's. They are unmarried. One will teach you cookery and the other accounts. Both may be of more value to you at Pless, I think, than Italian and the harp and the rest."

I sulked, thrusting out my underlip; I did not care for the thought of the two spinsters and the cookery. It would be as bad as being closeted with McLehose and Crindle together, and with no other company to relieve the boredom. Suddenly I realised how much I was going to miss the company of Mary and Raisin Pudding and the rest. My boxes were roped to the coach by now, and I looked up at the window for a last farewell; most of the twelve young ladies were there with their noses pressed against the glass, as I had seen them when I first came. Well, they would have observed for themselves that my husband was not seven feet high, but looked instead like other folk. I surveyed him covertly as the coach lumbered down the High Street. His looks, I decided, might have been worse.

# Fourteen

ANDREW's spinster relatives lived in what had once been two whitewashed cottages but were now one, making a long low house with a green space in front where hens pecked amiably. As soon as our carriage-wheels were heard one of the sisters came out; I observed her with some misgiving. She wore a drab-coloured gown, very old, with an apron and a cap on her grey hair. Her face was yellow with the tinge often attained by cottage-dwellers, I think as the result of living by a smoky fire and on sunny days sitting at the door. Like McLehose, she smiled to show a flash of china teeth. She bobbed to Andrew but did not kiss him. She was tiny, smaller than I. She did not reach Andrew's shoulder.

Inside the cottage there was a bright wood fire burning. Coming in out of the daylight I could make out the shape of a great black kettle steaming on it, hung by a hook. Nearby were a polished brass jelly-pan and a greased pancake girdle, and nearby again, a spinning-wheel and a quantity of carded wool in a basket. From amongst all these possessions rose the second sister, Miss Minney, who had been seated majestically doing nothing. She was taller and stouter than the other, Miss

Jule, and had a hooked nose. I learned later that she had been a governess for many years, being the only member of the family with enough health and strength to go out to work. All the rest had died of consumption. Miss Jule had nursed them and watched them die. She had no air of consequence or of duty well done; she might have been a servant in her own house. Miss Minney, as I was soon to learn, put on the show, and it was by her that I was to be taught accounts.

Both ladies pressed Andrew to stay for a meal, but he would not, saying he must return to Pless. Everyone clustered at the door to see him off. When he had gone, the two sisters relieved me of my cloak, which I still wore, and exclaimed at my dress, which they thought very fine. They also told me I was pretty, and stroked my cheek and sleeve. It was as though they had acquired a new and engaging pet. We sat down to a handsome meal of eggs, scones and butter and strong tea. I was given a barred chair with arms, and observed that they watched every mouthful as I ate, not as though they grudged it but as if something wonderful was happening. I later learned that they adored Andrew, whom they remembered from a child. I heard all manner of stories of his boyhood from them; how he would run away from lessons with his father, the dominie, and go out to help the shepherds in the lambing-season on the hills, and to shear the fleeces. "He was the despair of his father," they kept saying proudly, "but after he had rin awa'"—I took it this meant Canada—"he never failed to send money to his mother, poor soul, till, he died." Well, that was handsome to hear, and it was a revelation to me not to have Andrew taken for granted, as he had always been at Pless.

Now, however, I myself was the object of attention, and was to have my fill of it in the days that followed. We conversed politely for an hour, but I was tired after the journey and was beginning to feel miserable, as one usually is in a new place for the first day or two. Miss Minney said to Miss Jule, as one giving orders "Best show the wee thing till her room," and I knew that, however much she might ape gentility, she was kinder than McLehose. Miss Jule stood up and smoothed her apron, and Miss Minney then told me with pride that I was to have a room to myself. I was relieved; the conditions at the Lawnmarket had left me with a great longing for privacy, even after the few days spent by myself in lack of penitence in the punishment-room. Nor, I was certain, seeing the well-scoured pans, would there be fleas in the bed here. I was right; I slept that night in a soft bed stuffed with down (Miss Jule had stuffed it herself from birds she had plucked, and made the counterpane) and between sheets pleasantly dry and scented with lavender. I slept well, for it had been an eventful day.

Next morning Miss Jule appeared with a brass can full of hot water. I cannot begin to describe all the tasks she performed for myself and Miss Minney; we were not even allowed to darn our own stockings. Miss Minney, after a lifetime of this treatment, never lifted a finger, but she proved to be a good and apt teacher of arithmetic, and I soon began to improve mine. As for the cookery lessons, I had been wary about these and so, in her way, was Miss Jule; she did not like to have anyone else interfering with the kitchen. But she taught me how to make light pastry, and the way to keep it cool on a marble slab, and other things I would need to know "when I was feeding Andra at Pless". Andrew must be fed, and it occurred to me to wonder how he had managed all these years, for Bethia was an indifferent cook. Now I would be able to make nourishing broth from a bone, and all manner of things. Miss Minney sat, during the cookery-sessions, like a fat chick waiting to be crammed with food. She ate what we had made without comment, and did not help with the washing-up. Miss Jule had a fierce love for her as the last of the family; besides the darned hose, Miss Minney's linen would be washed, hung out on a bush to dry, and ironed with a flat-jack which stood always near the hearth. She herself never stirred a finger.

By the end, between the two of them, I would become as

conversant as any other housewife, and much more so than many a young bride, about the smooth running of an establishment. I would also be able to direct my servants, which is a thing not every female can do, so that they take advantage of her ignorance.

Time passed swiftly at the long house, and I was happy. When one is so there is little to say, but I soon came to love the sisters and, as a result, progressed faster than I had done with the accomplishments at McLehose's school. It seemed no time at all when I had been there a year. Andrew wrote sometimes to me and, now that my answers were no longer supervised, I replied as I chose. One day a letter came with different news. A widow-woman, who wanted to earn money for her fare to Lancashire for her son's wife's lying-in, had agreed to act as housekeeper at Pless for the months of July and August. Would I care to come home for the time and invite a friend for company?

I wrote joyfully to Mary, with whom I had been forbidden to correspond, and asked her. A reply came soon, smuggled out of the Lawnmarket school by way of the maidservant. Thereafter I could neither settle to cookery nor accounts, so full of excitement was I at the thought of seeing both Mary and Pless. How much we should have to tell one another! And I could show her how to bake tarts.

The sisters were wistful when I went off, and it occurred to me that I might have kissed them goodbye. But they were undemonstrative people, in the way the Scots sometimes are. It occurred to me then that I was married to a Scot. I felt that I knew much more about Andrew than before I had gone to live at the whitewashed house, and could perhaps tease him with tales of his boyhood, when he had—judging by the cousins' talk—been as much of a scapegrace as I.

# Fifteen

MARY HUGGED ME. "Oh, Primrose, everything has been so dull since you went away! If I could only tell you—" and she proceeded to do so, in the midst of the cobbled square where we changed coaches, and where it had been arranged that Andrew should escort the pair of us back to Pless while he rode his grey. The luggage was being hoisted from one coach to the other; straw blew about, and the post-horses were being given their water at the common trough; everyone was busy, and Andrew had for the moment gone over to see that our hampers and valises were not misdirected; he still held his mount by the rein. I had not had time to make the introduction between him and Mary.

"Did old McLehose agree to your coming to stay with me?" I asked curiously; I knew that Mary had come straight from Edinburgh.

"Oh, depend upon it she did not, but I smuggled out a letter to Mama, and she wrote that I was to be given permission. Fancy even having our letters read before we see them! How fortunate you are to be free of it, Primrose—you look well, you are prettier than ever—is that one of your farmers standing beside the grey mare's head? He is fixing us with a stare, as if he knew us both; why, of course it is your husband. I recall seeing him take you away from school."

I hastened to introduce Andrew, flushing a trifle with mortification that he should have been even briefly mistaken for a farmer. Certainly he looked like nothing more, with his plain dark clothes and skin freckled more than ever from working in the sun. Mary stared him up and down in a manner which one might have been pardoned for considering discourteous, as she was to be Andrew's guest. Once we were in the coach, she collapsed in giggles, and I regret to say I joined her; such is the effect of one foolish girl upon another, and I had no desire to quarrel with Mary at the outset.

The familiar ways drew on, and by evening we had come within sight of Pless. "Is that the lodge?" asked Mary. I blushed again; how was I to explain to this second cousin of a duchess that Pless boasted no lodges, and was set by itself? Clearly I had reason to be ashamed both of my house and my husband. It has occurred to me since then that perhaps unwittingly, at school, I had given the impression that Pless was larger and more important than it was. The coach set us down, and we left our baggage to be collected by the gate. At least, I thought, I had no reason to cry down the Tebb stone griffins, two of which, very old, flanked the gate-pillars. I pointed them out to Mary in a tone that left no doubt that lodges were for those newly come up in the world. I managed to sustain this attitude for the remainder of her stay.

What troubles me, even now, is my remembrance of our treatment of Andrew. The latter had, as usual, his mind fixed entirely on his trees, though I had seen him give a glance at me on seeing him again after leaving the spinster cousins, which showed that I did not displease him. Hence, either from his absence or dedication of mind, I think the full torments Mary and I would have put him to were largely spared him. From her first mistake about his identity, Mary made it clear he was a person to be made a butt of, and almost openly sympathised with me on my misalliance. It shames me to say that I let her keep this illusion, and myself bore no little part in ordering Andrew, as though he were a servant, and sniggering at his plain appearance and lack of fine manners. I knew within myself that he had the ways of a natural gentleman, but with the artificial sort he had no truck, and never would. Mary had seen, or thought she had seen, something of the fine world with her grand relations, and mercilessly imitated Andrew with his set face in absence, and when he was present was impudent, using the manners of a mistress to a servant. (I think she resented the fact that he would not flirt with her, having grown very expert in the use of her eyelashes despite the Lawnmarket ban.) I am ashamed to say that I took my tone from her, and made Andrew pay doubly for the fact that he had sent me to school supposedly to improve my social standing. Our youth could not excuse us; what we needed, the pair of us, was a taste of the birch.

Nevertheless Andrew heeded his trees more than either Mary or myself, and was out at them every morning by the time we descended for breakfast. They had grown so high that I exclaimed at sight of them, and Mary shuddered. "What a great noisome forest to have round about one! I don't envy you when you come to live here always," she said. "They cast a gloom even in the noon sunshine, when there is any." She was critical even of the weather at Pless, for since the trees had grown the rainfall increased, which Andrew told me was to be expected. "The trees will be cut down before I come," I answered her rather shortly. Truth to tell I did not know when Andrew would decide that I must come and live with him as his wife, and the prospect unsettled me.

But the trees meantime occupied his whole thought. On the first morning after our arrival I had jumped out of the bed I shared with Mary and ran to the window to look at the changed countryside; now I affected not to heed the wooded country where formerly there had been marsh. But one day Andrew said that we must come to see the queen tree. Mary announced however that she had the headache, and would rather not come; so I went alone. I was conscious of the great tall trunks pressing me in on every side, and when at last I came to the centre of the forest, there was a bronze-coloured tree and, high above, the beginnings of a seed-box. I turned to Andrew, and for once was civil with him. "You will be pleased," I said.

He was staring up at the tree-seed, and did not at once answer. Then he said, evenly, "Yes, it has been worth all the work," and turned away towards the hut, leaving me to find my own way back. Now I could see the purpose of the radial diggings; it was impossible to lose oneself in the forest. I raised my head and sniffed the air, close as it was and smelling of fir resin. The strange trees were not altogether like firs, being broader in the leaf. The paths were thick with the shed leaves of former years, making a dry carpet.

I returned to Mary, who was yawning with boredom in the house. "Has your headache gone?" I asked her. She said that it had, and I asked her if she would care to ride out, as it was a fine day. We dressed in our habits and went down together to the stables. There was no groom, which disturbed her high-and-mightiness, but before long we had got our own mounts saddled and bridled, and were off. I cantered towards the plantation; I was determined that Mary should admire it, in spite of herself.

The dew was still fresh on the turf in the trees' shadows, making the hoofbeats sound softly. Suddenly I heard a shriek of disgust from Mary. I wheeled about; had she hurt herself? It appeared not; she pulled at the reins and was away, faster than I could catch up, for I had given her the better pony of the two; my own dear old Pleasance was dead. I came up to her at last, waiting in a place where we could again see the house-walls. "Ugh," she said, "you didn't tell me you had a blackamoor. I can't endure 'em. I hope he does not come into the house?"

I bit my lip, realising that I should perhaps have said something to her about Saginaw before we came here; he was clearing undergrowth placidly, and had taken no heed of us. Had it indeed been true that at school I had never once spoken of him? I knew that it was, and knew the reason. I said to Mary, without apology, "Since you ask, he is not a blackamoor, but a half-Indian; his father was French. No, he does not enter the house. He shares the secret of growing these trees with my husband, and guards them always. Do not say, I beg you, to Andrew that you mislike him." I did not add that they were blood-brothers; she would only have been contemptuous. She set her nose in the air now.

"I am unlikely to mention the subject to anyone," she announced. I fell silent; had it been possible that I had defended Saginaw?

The holiday passed. Towards the end Andrew, weary no doubt of our ill-mannered ways, left us completely to our own devices. When it shone we were out, riding or walking, and when it rained we stayed indoors, chatting and eating sweet-meats by the fire. Andrew's housekeeper, a timorous soul, I think regarded us as a pair of hoydens, and seldom came near us, going about her duties quietly elsewhere. I thought of Miss Jule and how she was no doubt thinking of me as baking pastries for Andrew and helping to launder the sheets. Instead, I played cards with Mary. "I do not know how you can endure the prospect of living here," said the latter one day. She had grown in rudeness and I, being of weak character, let her do so, partly because she was my guest. However she flung down a hand of knaves and queens and said "Come to Maverick next year; I am invited, and there is always diversion there. They keep seven footmen as well as other staff, and there is constant gaiety, for my cousin the Duchess loves to be amused. Ask your dull stay-at-home Andrew if you may come."

"But will the Duchess welcome me?"

Mary fanned herself with the cards. "Oh, if I let her know that you are my friend, she will bid you come. There are thirty bedrooms for guests alone. It makes no odds for one more."

So I was bidden in due course to Maverick. For once in my life I would be glad to avoid Pless, as though Penuel's ghost walked about the house and grounds in the shadow of the great trees, trailing unhappiness. Also, I was in an undecided state about Andrew. He had said nothing about my returning to stay with the spinsters, and I would not ask him concerning it.

## Sixteen

THE VISIT TO PLESS had unsettled me, and although I was at
length returned to them I never again found myself able to
settle down with the good spinster ladies as before. There had
also been Mary's chatter about the great world, despite the
fact that she was not yet launched into society. She would see
it before long; unlike me, I reflected, and nursed my grievances
at being shut away, first in the Lawnmarket school and now
with two wardresses, for so my imagination unjustly painted
the sisters at this time. By now I was often pert with them, as
I had been with Andrew at Pless. Miss Minney may have had
experience with difficult schoolgirls during her governessing
years, and Miss Jule had a deal of unworldly wisdom, which
enabled them to put up with me. Certainly my discontent was
evident to them, and when I was more than usually fractious
or rude I would see them exchange eloquent glances one with
the other. They never uttered a word of reproach for the
annoyances I inflicted; some of these were physical, for I took
to going off on long wild walks about the countryside, and poor
Miss Minney used to pant by my side as chaperon. I did not
want her, but preferred to be alone with my thoughts, however

disagreeable these had become; and deliberately outpaced the poor lady in the knowledge that her whalebone stays encased her like a cage, not permitting her to walk easily with all of her body, but only to waddle like a duck that cannot bend at the waist. Our walks must have been a sore trial to her, and she would return bathed in sweat. Miss Jule never came, for she had too many tasks to leave her with time for walking.

One day, to my diversion, two letters came. One was from Andrew, who wrote regularly, and I put it aside and opened the other first. To my joy it was from Mary, who said that her cousin the Duchess of Croy was about to write to Andrew to ask if I might visit Maverick with Mary at the next summer holiday. I could hardly contain my excitement; the great world at last! It was some time before I remembered to read Andrew's letter; with or without his permission, I was thinking, I would somehow contrive to go to Maverick.

This was the letter, which I read then.

*My Dear Wife, I write to let you know that the Plantings have largely done as we Hoped and the Seed Box on the Queen Tree looks well and should grow. This gives me a Trifle more Leisure to pay heed to you and to our Marriage, which I have sadly Neglected. It is indeed Time that you became my Wife in Truth. I look to hear from you on this, and to say when you wish that I should come and fetch you from where you now are. Pray give my Compliments to the Cousins. You should be Proficient by now in all Accomplishments, including the Baking of Bread which I shall be glad to see, we here having nothing to eat but flat Stuff Bethia makes now Mrs. Lytham is Departed to Lancashire. For other Reasons Also, it would give me Pleasure to see you here. I must haste now to send this off. I look to hear from you, and remain your Devoted Husband, A. Farquharson.*

I slammed down the letter on the table and burst into tears. The good ladies, who were both in the room, hurried over to ask what ailed me, and at that strange moment I realised that they were truly fond of me and that all my ill temper and sullens had gone for naught. While I wiped my eyes I was thinking already what my plan should be. "Oh, Andrew wants me to go to Pless and Mary has invited me to stay at Maverick House with her cousin the Duchess, and I cannot be in both places, and I wanted to see the world." Tears overcame me again at the last utterance; to my secret triumph Miss Minney bridled and said that to be sure, I must accept the Duchess's invitation; Andrew would not be unreasonable. I had judged correctly, little wretch that I was, that a title would have a magical effect on Miss Minney. Miss Jule said nothing.

"She will need some gowns," said Miss Minney, and then I knew the battle was won. I was in fact still wearing those I had had at school, whose hems had been let down but which were now too tight about the bosom.

I was glad of my accomplices. While Miss Minney herself sat down and took pen and paper to advise Andrew, in her small fine handwriting, that it would be a shame if I missed this chance, I wrote on my account likewise and we enclosed one letter inside the other to save the post. Mine ran *My Dear Husband, Wait until after the Summer, because I have an invitation from the Dutchess to stay at Maverick, which I am sure you would not have me Miss as I shall meet the Polite World there, and can perhaps try out my Harp you paid for, and my French.* I did not know, or care, if there were a harp at Maverick; but there was no harm in reminding Andrew he had paid for a genteel education for me and that this was an opportunity of airing it.

A reply came from him in a day or two, on reading through which I guessed he was hurt. But I did not care, and by now, assuming his permission, I was busying myself over the matter of the new gowns, and had sent for stuff from Edinburgh out of a book of pattern-samples. Miss Jule being a notable dress-maker (there was in fact very little she could not do) she cut and pinned and fitted the cloth when it came, and I exerted myself to help with the hems. By the end of our labours there was a becoming green watered satin and a French velvet of a wine colour for cooler days, as well as sundry pretty summer gowns in pastel shades. I also sent for a bonnet-shape and Miss Jule helped me to cover and trim it with matching bunched ribands or rosettes of straw. I was very well set out by the end, and was sure nobody at Maverick would be better dressed. It also pleased me that I had had the less time to reflect upon Andrew and his demands. Truth to tell, I was very much afraid of them.

## Seventeen

MAVERICK IS NOT an old house, having been built only in the last reign out of the immense fortune the first Duke amassed by luck at cards and judicious investment. It is plainer and more sprawling than Chatsworth or Longleat, as well as lacking their histories. However when I saw it for the first time I was greatly impressed and the sight of the massive pillared portico, three times the size of ours at Pless, dwarfed me in my own estimation. I began to wonder if the gowns made by Miss Jule would suit; there were ladies and gentlemen parading up and down the walk in front of the house, pausing at the great stone urns to admire the flowers that brimmed over there in the sunshine, or standing on the low flight of steps that led to a sunken lawn in the centre of which stood a sundial. Their clothes were enviable, of the finest materials and cut, and their hair was powdered though it was still day.

Scarcely less impressive were the footmen, two of whom seized our baggage and bore it away as if it spoilt the scene; I began to wonder if we would ever see it again. I stole a glance at Mary, who looked nonchalant and kept her nose in the air, so I did the same; and thus we were led through great entry-rooms with polished floors and statues in niches, more flowers disposed in baskets and vases, and corridors whose carpeted length seemed endless. In the end we were shown our rooms and an apology was made to us that we would be obliged to share a maid, as the house was so full. I had never before had a personal maid, and the prospect alarmed me; what if she should sneer at my dresses? I was glad at least that I was sharing her with Mary, whose room was next to mine.

I looked about the room, which was less notable than those we had passed through, not much grander in fact than my own room at Pless, though the bed-curtains were done in Spanish blackwork. There was a wash-stand and commode and two gilt chairs, which had perhaps seen better days in the drawing-room, and a small sofa on which, no doubt, I could lie when indisposed. However I had begun to feel more cheerful and after washing myself, I went to the window to look out at whatever view should present itself to me. It was yet some time till dinner, and I did not know what else to do.

At first I was delighted; behind the house was a maze, as high and dark as that at Hampton Court, which I have since heard of: it must have been much older than the house. I stared at it, and at once saw that two gentlemen, one in uniform, were disporting themselves by chasing a maid-servant, who had evidently lost her way among the high yew walls. Her cries came dimly through the glass of my casement, and I could see her; she was a little plump rosy-cheeked thing in a grey gown and mob cap, no doubt from the kitchens. As I watched, one of the men caught her and gave her two smacking kisses on the mouth, and began to pull at her bodice. She tore herself away, and ran round into the arms of the other, who by this time I had been astonished to see was my cousin Thornton. What was he doing here? How had he received the invitation? Did Mary know? All these questions chased one another through my mind, even as the two fine gentlemen continued to chase the poor little maid. Every time she tried to make her way out it was to fall into the embrace of one or the other, for the men obviously knew the maze and its ways much better than she did. In the end, as I watched, she was caught for good by the other assailant, a tall fellow with wild hair and eyes, and he proceeded to have his way with her unhindered. I felt the small shrieks and cries she was emitting, and turned from the window, feeling faint; were all men such beasts?

At this moment there was a discreet knock on the door, and there was the abigail. A kind of wild inward laughter beset me; had she also been chased through mazes and deflowered? If it had happened it must have been a long time ago; she was a thin elderly woman, with the marks of a lifetime's service in her gait and expression; in a colourless voice she asked which gown I would have laid out for dinner, and offered to dress my hair. I sat down to let her do this, and while I was under her ministrations in came Mary, already dressed in the yellow gown she had worn long ago on our jaunt in Edinburgh. This cheered me, for I at least had new ones, and eventually chose one of the pastels, which Havergal—this was her name —took away to iron the parts which were crushed. I waited on in my stays and petticoat, and whispered to Mary of what I had seen. She was still nonchalant, and laughed at my shock.

"Maids? Yes, they always get chased in the maze; 'tis their own fault for being lured into it." She took a look out of the window. "Why, that's Clun my cousin has taken her; best be careful of him, Primrose; he always makes a play for a new girl. He is married, and his wife's here in the house; you will meet her at dinner. Thornton? No, how should I know he had been invited? He may have come here through Clun himself, who goes north often. We will ask him when we see him. Everyone has gone from below now; you need have no fear."

And indeed the maze was now unpopulated, but I never afterwards looked upon it without a feeling of discomfort. However there was little time to repine, for Havergal reappeared to dress me for dinner, and by the time she had finished with me I daresay I looked as well set out as Mary, whose dark straight hair did not take well to curling-tongs and already hung limp. We had not asked for powder, being too young.

When it was time to go down to dinner Mary came for me and together we approached the grand staircase. It was at once graceful and massive, being fashioned of marble, and forming a double twisted spiral. Now and again, at regular intervals, statues embellished it. Before we had got very far Mary pulled me behind one which I later learned was a life-sized bust of the first duke, taken in his dotage. His full periwig with its marble curls protected us while we looked down at the assembled company through the balusters; trust Mary to know of a point of vantage! It reminded me of my adventure long ago with the apples at Pless.

She indicated to my ignorance the people I had best meet. The extraordinary figure of the Duchess, our hostess, stood out in the throng. She was more than six feet tall, stout, and heavy-browed like a man; her massive arms were encased in diamond bracelets which sparkled in reflection of the light from the chandeliers. She was talking in a lazy way to the man I knew already to be Lord Harry Clun, and Thornton stood close by, pressing his advantage where he could. Nearby was a plain young woman, unbecomingly dressed in green; the gown was beautiful and very rich, but her sallow skin spoiled it. "That is Lady Harry," whispered my mentor. "She's as dull as a governess, which is why Clun has affairs. By her, the one standing in lavender silk, is an heiress." The heiress I thought was ugly, and must have been out for several seasons. "Then over there—you see, by the flowers?—that is Cousin Edith, who is the artist of the family; she draws and paints all day, with her sister." I stared down at the artist's withered frame; she was an old woman and seemed to take no interest in the company about her; she wore plumes in her grey hair, and carried a fan. "The other twin, Cousin Matilda, takes fits, and is never seen in company. Edith stays by her all day."

"Drawing?" I asked. Mary nodded with assurance.

"Oh, yes, they both draw. Perhaps that is why Edith was never married, though nothing's wrong with *her* wits. Do you see the exquisite who is trying to establish himself with the heiress I told you of? That is—"

But I was never to know who the corseted and elderly exquisite, in his maroon coat and ruffles, might be, for he was not one of the house-party and I never saw him again after that night. Meantime the Duchess had caught sight of us and beckoned us, with an imperious motion, to descend the stairs and show ourselves.

We went, with skirts held correctly and heads high; but of all that richly dressed company I was chiefly aware of one, and he unwelcome. Lord Harry Clun had fixed his pale wild gaze firmly on me from the first, and although I preserved my demeanour I had no wish to become acquainted with him. But the Duchess's deep voice—where was the Duke, I wondered innocently? Later I learned that he lived always in London, with a plain and devoted mistress—Her Grace's voice made us welcome, and introduced me, as Mrs. Farquharson, to the hot gaze of Clun, the tolerant one of my cousin Thornton (he had come, as Mary had guessed, at Clun's suggestion) and the hostile one of Lady Harry, alert already in her expensive grass-green gown.

Afterwards we all went in to dinner.

# Eighteen

I FIND THAT I notice any new acquaintance first by the eyes, and that first evening at Maverick I had plenty of scope for this indulgence. The Lady Edith with her plumes sat opposite me, and her gaze was unnerving, at once grey and bright. I do not think that during the course of the entire meal she took her glance from me except occasionally to lower it to her plate. At first I assumed that this was due to a kind of ill-breeding which is at times met with in high circles, and tried to ignore it by looking at my other neighbours and now and again replying to them when they spoke. My discoveries were various; the Duchess herself, under her mannish brows, had a heavy-lidded, worldly gaze out of eyes the colour of onyx, which she seldom opened wide. I had the feeling that she did not miss a jot of what went on about the long table, and that she put her conclusions tidily away in a place in her mind kept for them, for use later. I felt, even then, that she should have been a man; she cannot have been a comfortable person to whom to be married, though I came to have a great regard for her as a friend and was glad of her like regard for me. But all that was to come later; meantime, I had to parry glances from

Clun which were full of pale fire, and occasional amused ones
from Thornton when he was not occupied with the heiress,
next to whom good fortune, or design, had placed him. Young
as I was I remember thinking how provident such a union
would prove for Thornton, who liked to live well and had
nothing but his army pay, so that he was, as I already suspected, heavily in debt. Perhaps Clun's acquaintance would
turn out to be his salvation, but I did not think it would be
mine, and all through dinner—the courses were good, varied
and elaborate, ending with a lemon syllabub as light as air—
I endeavoured to avoid his gaze, which made me self-conscious
when I looked elsewhere and spoilt my enjoyment of what
would otherwise have been an elevating experience; I had
never hoped to see so rich an assembly, and there was much wit
bandied about the table which I have forgotten. I did not once
think of Andrew, alone at Pless.

But I must return to what happened with the Lady Edith.
I had come to the conclusion that she was mad, like her sister,
with her constant staring at me; then I saw the Duchess look
from one to the other of us and surprised a flicker, no more,
of discernment in her half-shut eyes. After dinner we went
into the card-room, for there was to be no dancing that night
(for which I was thankful) and I expected that Mary and I
would be suffered to retire early, for we were tired after the
journey and much the youngest of anyone there. But it was not
to be. The Duchess herself, before she sat down at a table for
whist, swept me along with her to where the Lady Edith was
standing, looking like a heron in search of fish, or so I thought.
When I was brought to her, she clasped her hands and studied
me for some instants with her head on one side, so that the
plumes wavered.

"Pure Greuze," she said, "do you not think so, Dorothea?"
But the Duchess, so addressed, declined to comment, merely
shaking her head good-naturedly and saying "You may hazard
more as to that than I, as you know well," and retired to her

card-table. I was left, somewhat at a loss, with the Lady
Edith, who had begun to caress and stroke me with old, dry,
freckled hands, as though I had been a new acquisition;
perhaps, for all I knew to the contrary, she had meant I was
like some bird. Our genteel education in the Lawnmarket had
not included the history of modern art, and I had never before
heard of Greuze and did not even connect him with painting.
Since then I have found, as I said earlier, that he paints very
young girls with dark curly hair and features not unlike mine,
and arouses desire in the beholder through some feature of an
otherwise innocent appearance. I cannot explain myself
better than to say that it was not entirely a compliment to have
been compared to a Greuze. It admitted some moral defect
in me, while allowing that I was pretty.

I escaped from the Lady Edith's pattings at length, but not
before she had told me "We will meet again; *must* meet again.
You shall come to us in the pavilion."

I had no idea what she could mean, and having thankfully
escaped I looked about to catch Mary's eye and ask our hostess
if we might go to bed. No doubt it was not etiquette to do so,
but by now I could hardly stand on my feet. Such was high
life. I did not think then that I wanted more than a glimpse
of it; but as the days passed I was to begin to feel very differently.

Next morning, as Havergal brought in my chocolate, a folded
note lay on the tray. "May we expect you in the pavilion this
morning?" it said. I knew it was from the Lady Edith, and so
evidently did Havergal, when I asked her where the pavilion
might be found. The maid proved to be at once helpful and
kind, and she said to me "Never heed dress greatly, at this
hour, miss; none of 'em is about afore noon, except the Duchess
at her roses. Go past her—she'll take no heed—and cross the
low lawn and turn to the left, and there is the little pavilion
all of glass, where the two old ladies work, and have their meals
sent, that is when they're busy."

With her help I put on a morning-wrapper and combed my
hair. The chocolate had been delicious and pleasantly hot,
and the silver jug and cup smooth with age and very beautiful.
I had noticed many things which showed that a connoisseur's
taste, such as I knew of it, was at work in the great ugly house.
I supposed it to be the Duchess's. She certainly had the air of
knowing what she wanted, and no doubt could pay for it.

I saw her, as Havergal had forewarned me, out at the rose-
garden in an old chip-straw hat and a wrapper such as I
myself wore, and carrying a flat basket which she was filling
with the withered heads of roses. "A good morning to you,"
she called as I went past, and I made my curtsy. "These aren't
too far gone for pot-pourri; it does as well with withered
flowers as fresh." She seemed taken up with her task, and I
crept past and found the pavilion, its multitude of panes gleam-
ing in the morning sun. A creeper of some kind shaded it on one
side, and it had a miniature dome.

The Lady Edith had espied me and opened the door.
"Welcome, shepherdess," she cried, and I began to think that
she was more than ever mad. I curtseyed a second time, and
again a third to the other who stood in a corner with her back
to the light, holding a pad and a pencil. She did not speak,
then or later; it was Lady Edith who made all the talk. Before
very long I knew what they wanted of me, though I had never
heard of the occupation before; I was to be a model, for the
sisters to draw and perhaps paint. Lady Edith was greatly
excited. She arranged me in a pose on a low stool, and presently
opened my wrapper and drew down my shift. I protested somewhat, at which she laughed; many things seemed to amuse her.

"Have no fear, the world doesn't pass by here," she said.
"With so pretty a model we should like to draw her at times as
nature has made her. Surely you will not grudge us this
little pleasure? Perhaps when you see the first drawing, you
will agree—there, a little further round to face the shoulder.
So! Keep still if you can, and fix your eyes on a spot beyond the

glass. Does that suit you, Matilda?"

Matilda said nothing, but sat down and started to draw. I sat in my abandoned pose, feeling some embarrassment lest anyone should come to look in at the door or the many windows; then as time passed I realised that no one would. I knew, also, that I was beginning to be cruelly cramped, and I longed to stretch my limbs and change my position. I believe Lady Edith had forgotten the time, for she was drawing as busily as her sister. In the end they showed me the drawings; they were good, and I realised that in these two queer lonely old ladies there was talent, if not genius, here within the house of glass. I gladly offered to pose for them again on the morrow "but, please, may I rest a little while during it?" Then Lady Edith was full of self-reproach; I had been so good a model that she had quite forgotten the time, and I should have rested every quarter-hour. "Tomorrow, if I don't recall it, remind me, my dear." I said that I would, and entered upon my apprenticeship with some pleasure—it is always flattering to be the centre of attention—and some good-humour and more doubt; I did not want to be caught in my morning-wrapper, hurrying back across the grass, by Clun or another. But, as Havergal had said, nobody stirred at Maverick before noon.

The task I had undertaken in becoming the two sisters' model prolonged my stay long past the time I had expected, and even Mary had gone back to her people as her father was ill. I missed her less than I had thought I would do; the days were filled with pleasure, and I had made new friends. The Duchess herself often spoke to me, seemed pleased with my answers, and said she was glad that I had agreed to oblige her sisters-in-law. "They have little in their lives, and this is a joy to them," she told me, and I flushed at the praise.

Thornton however was not so pleased with me. One day he sought me out, between changing tables at cards, for I played by now most nights. He said "Primrose, will you not

oblige me by being a little civil to Clun? I owe him a good
deal, y'know, and he favours my suit." The last he did not
have to explain, for his pursuit of Miss Desmond, the heiress,
had assumed serious proportions and from his air and speech, I
gathered that he had hope of winning her, except for me.
"Why, I am as civil as I need be for my own protection," I
said sharply, but I knew I had not, in fact, given Clun anything
except discouragement, either over the fans of cards when his
eyes sought mine, or on other occasions. I had danced in a
quadrille with him once, but the exertions of that do not allow
for eye-play, much less lovemaking. Otherwise I had avoided
him when I could. But he still followed me, and was an embarrassment as I felt not the least liking for him, and was certain
his wife resented me through no fault of my own. Why could
not Thornton contrive his own affairs without recourse to me?
I told him as much. "You got me into great trouble in
Edinburgh, and would do the same here," I said. "Do you
think me a fool? The very first day I came I saw the pair of
you disport yourselves with a servant in the maze, and you
think to do the same with me; well, you shall not." And I
turned and left him, and went to my new table, but could not
thereafter concentrate on the cards, and lost the game. Truth
to tell I was fond enough of Thornton, and would have wished
him well in his search for a rich wife. I reminded myself that
he was Penuel's brother and that therefore I had a duty
towards him. Perhaps if I made myself pleasant to Miss
Desmond, that would help. I tried, but she only stared at me
out of her watery blue eyes, and I do not think she followed
half I said. She had neither wit nor beauty, but much money,
for her father owned coal-mines in Yorkshire. It said little for
her that, with all this, she was not married long before now;
but it was none of my business.

That night I penned a letter to Andrew, of whom I sometimes thought as a stranger met with long ago, in another
world. "*There are such Diversions here, that I believe I shall stay a*

*While until the Water Party is over, which takes place next week.
There is still much Company here. I hope your Trees do well.*"I signed
this and sent it down to the Duchess for franking, without
giving a further thought to my husband except that it seemed a
long time since I had heard from him, but it did not trouble me
greatly. Truth to tell I was putting off the return to Andrew
and the taking up of my duties as a wife, which still frightened
me. I could not explain this to anyone, because even had I had
so close a friend as could have advised me on it, I could not
have revealed the information concerning Penuel, which was
the cause of my fear. So I kept silent, except that I played a
full part in the diversions I had written of to Andrew, and
danced and drank wine and played whist and was rowed up
and down on the artificial lake, though never with Clun to
escort me unless there were others present. There were bright
foreign fish in the lake which would rise to be fed with cake-
crumbs, and lilies with great broad leaves whereon the water
sat in beads, for they were waxy. It was pleasant to be rowed
there and to trail one's fingers in the water, and to pretend
that one was both rich and noble and that this visit would
never come to an end.

Clun himself played the next card. One morning I was
sitting for my old ladies, mercifully draped, for they were
studying and drawing folds and the way they fell. I reflected
that I had posed as almost every classical nymph in the
calendar; naked as Niobe, weeping and kneeling; relaxed as
Ariadne, waking from sleep to find that Theseus has left her;
abandoned as Leda, to whom a swan was supposedly making
love. This was a drawing I was somewhat ashamed of, for I
had had to sit leaning back a trifle, with my legs open. To my
relief Lady Edith announced that this drawing was lost. She
did not seem troubled, and as the studio was always in chaos
neither was I. Suddenly I saw, from my bedraped position, a
pair of pale eyes watching me from behind the creeper that
grew on the south side. I screamed, and clutched my draperies

to me. Lady Edith ran out, drawing-paper in hand.

"Go away, you ignoble man! Go away! Go away!" I saw the figure of Clun retreat while she pursued him, and while the sight must have been comic I was too greatly upset, both at the late happening and at my being left for the first time alone with Lady Matilda, who was strange that day, that I burst into tears. Lady Matilda replied by falling down in a fit, which occupied Lady Edith fully when she returned, and I left my posing for the day and thankfully got on my wrapper and went back to my room. Later in the day Clun trapped me in a corner, and seeing my haughty look begged my pardon. The Duchess herself, he indicated, had bidden him apologise; she had heard about the whole episode from Lady Edith.

"But I wish I had come some other day, when you were not clad," he murmured, and I flushed indignantly. "Indeed, sir, if that thought is in your mind I cannot continue to sit for the ladies at all," I told him, but he appeared to care nothing and only said, with his hand on the place where his heart should have been had he had one, "Ah! If I might beg but one kiss from that pair of rogue's lips, even that would content me . . . for the time. When may I see you alone, Mrs. Farquharson? Since the first night I saw you, coming down those stairs, with your dark curls and child's face and the little tits thrusting out against your gown, I have wanted nothing and no one else. Can you not have pity?"

But I turned and left him.

The Duchess sent for me and informed me that, owing to Clun's imprudence, it would be better if I ceased my sittings for the time. "They will be disappointed, it is true," she said, regarding her sisters-in-law, "but after all we can hire a model for them, who will not be compromised. There is a young girl in the kitchens who might suit."

The one who was chased and caught in the maze, I thought; no doubt Clun, having had all he wanted of her, would not trouble *her* sittings. I felt miserable, and said to the Duchess "Madam, it would be best perhaps if I end my stay, before I tire you," although I did not relish the idea of going back to Pless, and missing the water-party. Some of this must have shown on my face, for the Duchess said, with her hooded eyes kindly, "Why, child, you must stay to take part in the junketings; they would not be the same without you, for you make a pretty sight and cheer many eyes besides those of Harry Clun. He is a fool, and his own enemy; pay no heed to him."

## Nineteen

THE WEATHER continued fine, and plans were set on foot for the water-party in three days' time; the servants were already threading coloured lanthorns among the trees on the island in the artificial lake. Company was to come from far and near, and we would all wear masks and dominoes; I had been given mine, of a violet colour, and they hung expectantly in my room. I had never been to such an entertainment and looked forward to it with excitement; from what I had heard, it would be like Venice, with its waterways and music from gondolas, masked ladies and incognito gallants. However I would know Harry Clun by his thin height, and would avoid him.

Lady Harry's demeanour puzzled me in those days. For some time she had been almost smug, except for the anxious glances with which she followed her errant lord's every movement while he was in her sight, which was seldom. Now, however, she had red eyes, as though she had been weeping. Clun himself was nowhere in sight. I said nothing of it to anyone except Havergal, who had become my confidante. She snorted as she tidied my things.

"They had a terrible set-to, his lordship and her ladyship,

that Barney the footman heard, and said my lord hurried out o' the room and down to stables and ordered his horse, then went gallopin' off to perdition, if you'll excuse the expression, ma'am. 'Tis nothing new for them to have words, but he always comes back, for it's her money they live on. Mr. Thornton Milhall's suit fares something better, so I'm told."

I smiled and said nothing, for I did not want to allow Havergal to become too familiar, though I was glad of her snippets of news, which kept me from making myself foolish in the drawing-room or at the dining-table. However she chattered on. "Barney said the Cluns had words over a pitcher, but what it meant he couldn't be sure, Lord Harry comin' out about then."

My cheeks grew hot, for I knew at once that the picture in question could only be the lost Leda, and if Harry Clun had got hold of it I would never feel at ease in his presence again. I dismissed Havergal rather sharply, and she tossed her head on leaving; perhaps she would bring me no more news, but I would rather have had none than what I had had. I sat down and covered my crimson face with my hands. Then I decided there was, after all, nothing to do but behave as usual; if Clun had purloined the drawing it was his fault and not mine, although if he showed it about I thought I should die. But I had the notion that he would not, but would keep it for his own edification in private. Well, it was all he should have of me.

That night there was blind man's buff, for some members of the party felt childish. We all played, even the Duchess consenting to have her eyes covered with a linen kerchief, and her big form lurched about seeking a quarry. I noticed that Harry Clun had not returned from his ride, and no doubt was staying away from the house in a fit of pique. It was pleasanter without him.

The Duchess caught and guessed me, and after that I was blind man and in the end I caught Thornton, for I could feel the frogging on his coat. It occurred to me to wonder in that instant if he had indefinite leave from the army; he had been here longer than I had. Perhaps the Duchess had exerted her influence, which must mean she favoured his suit. His hopes of the heiress were now widely known, and some in the party had even entered bets on the matter. I suffered the kerchief to be untied from my head and tied it round Thornton's in his turn, and went back to the play.

Shortly afterwards the footman, not Barney but another, came to me and whispered in my ear that there was a message for me. I thought it must be from Clun and frowned, but what the man had to say was stranger still; yet I had no reason to disbelieve him.

"There is word from your husband, madam, and he begs that you will meet him in the summer-house, and say nothing to anyone of his being here."

"My—" But one did not argue with or question a servant in such ways; I slipped out of the room, not troubling to take a wrap for the night was warm, and made my way across the moonlit lawn in the opposite direction to that I had been used to take to the ladies and their pavilion. The noise of the house-party grew fainter. It did not occur to me to hide in the shadows of the sunken garden to disguise my errand; why should I not go to meet my own husband? No doubt Andrew was shy of such company, and would not come into the house.

The summer-house—some still called it a folly—was small and stood by itself away from the trees, so that if one had nothing better to do on a fine day one could sit in it, shading one's face from the sun. It was made of wood and had a ceiling of inlaid pine-cones, which smelled pleasant in the day's warmth. At this hour, however, it would be dank and cold. I resolved to try to bring Andrew to his senses and get him to come to the house, and meet the company.

What a fool I was! Had I taken but a moment's reflection, there was no way in which Andrew could have known of the folly's existence. But I went up to it without suspicion, and had none while I knocked on the door and called "Andrew?" and the door was flung open, then shut fast again with me inside—and beside me Harry Clun.

"How dare—" I was beginning, but he had seized and began kissing me. I could smell spirits on his breath and had time to reflect angrily that he must have spent the day drinking at some inn, compounding this infamous plot. I struggled, but he had put down the latch which shut the door from inside, and there was no hope of my reaching it. He was determined to have me, and that quickly; already his free hand fumbled at my dress, and had the bodice unlaced.

"Goddess. Torment. You have given me no peace of mind or body, and for that you shall pay." A kiss stopped his speech and my reply, and he crushed his mouth against mine and scooped up my skirts. I was struggling madly, but his imprisoning arm was strong and the other swift. I knew too well what would happen, and I could not cry out with his mouth on mine and my voice thereby stopped, and I—

"Open the door!"

It was a man's shout; blows were already hammering on the wood. Somehow, in the instant's surprise Clun was occasioned, I wrenched apart from him and lifted the latch and pulled open the door, and fell out, with my breasts bare, straight into Andrew's arms. He put a cloak about me—I saw dully that it was my own—and still keeping me close with his right arm dealt what I have sometimes heard described as a straight left to Clun, who took it on the jaw and fell back, hitting his head against the seat in the summer-house, and then lay still. He lay there dimly outlined by the moon. I spared an instant to wonder if he was dead, but it did not seem greatly to matter. For that moment, for the first time, Andrew filled my life. I wondered how he had known to come here.

# *Twenty*

ANDREW WAS very angry. It occurred to me with an odd clarity that I had never seen him angry before. The fact itself seemed to overshadow the late assault I had escaped, the mystery of Andrew's arrival, everything; I obeyed unquestioningly everything he would have me do. I suppose that I was still in shocked acquiescence. I can remember pulling my bodice together under the cloak he had brought, to give myself some appearance of decency.

He had me by the elbow. His grip was not soft, and I remember how he led me round past the shrubbery and rose-garden to where a carriage waited in the yard, without bringing me back past the house again. I recognised the Admiral's equipage from Pless. What had Andrew been about? How had he known to come for me? My mind began to thaw; I recall saying in a small voice "My things—my gear." Andrew said "I have arranged for it to be sent after us," and I knew then that there was no chance, even, of farewells.

"The Duchess—"

"I have left word for the Duchess. Make an end to such talk." He helped me in, if shovelling me in hostile fashion can be so described; and got himself in after me, for this time he had not brought his own mount to ride alongside. He sat in the corner of the coach, glaring at me; I knew this from the one scared glance I threw him, and then looked away. I dared say nothing, dared not even explain how I had come to be in the summer-house, alone with Clun. Who would believe me? Certainly not this stranger who sat opposite, and judged me in silence. I began to weep. He made no move, either to comfort or assist me.

We came to an inn. Andrew made me get out and I heard him instruct the coachman to find a groom and unharness the horses. That meant we were here for the night. I clutched at my cloak with my two hands, feeling as if it covered me naked. What would become of me now? Why must Andrew make me so afraid? I dried my tears with a fist; I did not want the servants at the inn to see me dishevelled and crying. I also discovered that I was hungry. It seemed a long time since dinner at Maverick and I realised we had since covered many miles. I had no notion of the time; it must be late.

Andrew came back from instructing the coachman and said to me "Pull your hood over your head, and keep silent till I bid you speak." His tone was that of a master to a servant, or perhaps a dog. I began to tremble. As though he knew this, but would not help me, he guided me inside the inn where he ordered a room for the night. I felt near to fainting, but the inn-folk knew him and addressed him by his name. There would be no aid for me from them, I knew.

The upstairs room was small, lit by candles in sconces. Andrew shut the door behind us as soon as the maid had withdrawn. He said "Take off your things." I removed the cloak. "Not only that; your clothes. You were almost naked earlier this evening. It should not be difficult to undress yourself a second time."

"Andrew, I—"

"Do as I say. I have it in mind to thrash you, but I would prove your guilt first. Come, hasten." He watched, leaning always against the door, while I undid my laces and let my gown slide to the floor, and took my shoes off. I was left in my petticoat and shift and stays, and try as I would I could not get the stay-laces to unfasten; Havergal must have tied them too firmly. I thought of Havergal and began to cry again, wrestling with the damned stays, and then Andrew strode over with an impatient catch of his breath, and ripped them open and off me. I can remember little more except his lifting me bodily and throwing me on the bed, where I hit my head against the bed-post, but I could not cry any harder than I was crying already. He said abruptly "Stop your noise," and turned away to undress himself. I hid my face in the pillows, full of shame; I was naked, and Andrew could see me by candlelight and had not troubled to snuff the sconces. If I were to ask him to put out the lights he would not. He would do nothing I asked of him, being too angry with me because Clun and I had been in the summer-house and he thought Clun was my lover.

I had misjudged Andrew. Methodically, he went round the sconces and pinched the wicks, a thing one can only do without burning the fingers when one is cool. Andrew was as cold as ice. When he came to bed in the darkness he flung himself on top of me and took me, not gently. I might have been a whore. The bed shook. I can remember thinking "They will know in the kitchen what we are at, because the kitchen is below," and then I felt a sharp thrusting pain and cried out loudly, and afterwards Andrew grew gentle and had lost his anger, but at the time I did not think why. I cried more tears into that pillow than ever in the whole of my life, even for Penuel. It was the same as Penuel and the Indian had been doing in the wood, I knew, what we were doing now. I would never be free of that memory, nor the shame of it. I felt as desolate as if a stranger had ravished me. I cried on until in the end I fell asleep.

Next day I woke heavy-eyed, and what awakened me was

Andrew's kissing. He kissed my mouth and my breasts and stomach, and then began to ride me again although I was still unwilling. By the time the maid came to the door to ask if we would have breakfast sent up I was tumbled and dishevelled, and hating my husband. I turned my head away while he called to the girl to bring up food and when it came I would eat nothing. He tried to coax me, saying "Primrose, Primrose, there will be no thrashing. I did not believe you were virgin; you see, a letter came—"

I said I did not want to listen and he fell silent and ate his food, unfeelingly as I thought, watching him wash it down afterwards with small-ale. He had hurt me; my body throbbed within itself and my arms were covered with bruises, and all he could do was eat. Presently he laughed and said "Get dressed, sweetheart, I'll tie your stay-laces, it's time we put the horses to and travelled on. I promised the Admiral he should have his carriage back today."

So the Admiral knew. In this, as in many things, I wronged Andrew. I began sullenly to dress myself and washed my face in cold water at the ewer; I would not permit Andrew to tie my stays, and he shrugged and laughed and said he would go down instead to pay the shot. By the time he had returned I had contrived to knot them, and was dressed and ready to enter the carriage. I did not say a word to Andrew on the journey. I was thinking of Maverick and that the day after tomorrow would be the water-party, and I would not be there.

## Twenty-one

WE EXCHANGED very few words on the final stage of the coach-journey: this was prudent because of the presence of the coach-man, who always hears more than many people assume. On alighting at Pless Andrew paid him and gave him ale-money, and shortly I heard the coach trundle off again back to the Admiral.

Taken up with my own thoughts as I was, I could not help but see that Pless was well-kept compared to what it had been. Over the last few years, as and when he could, Andrew had been improving it by slow stages. He had done a great deal with his own hands, besides engaging casual workmen. By now the stonework was newly pointed outside and plastered within, so that the very hall seemed fresh and large instead of a place of shadows. My father's chair still stood by the grate, in which a fire had been laid but not lit. Bethia had been waiting to curtsy us in; I went straight on up to my room, where she followed me. She had altered less than the house. When we were alone I flung myself on her shoulder and wept and wept.

She comforted me, while not approving the reason for my tears. "Why, ma'am, all men are so. Is it not a mercy ye have so good a man, as won't go a-whorin' or drink too much of nights? A steady worker, Mr. Andrew is, and has brought good to the neighbourhood as well as bringin' on them trees. I pray they may bring him the fortin he's hopin'. Keeps all of us well paid, Mr. Andrew does, and that reg'lar."

I could see there was no turning her from Mr. Andrew, so I went to the window where my tears could flow unheeded, as I had thought. However I was soon induced to dry them by the sight of the dark tall trees, like ranks of soldiers, incredibly grown since I had last seen them a year ago. Suddenly I hated them; I felt they were closing me in, would grow and creep ever nearer until they had smothered Pless, myself, everything I remembered. I hated Andrew also, I kept telling myself. Behind me I heard Bethia pouring water for me to wash. She waited on me while I did so, and I dabbed at my eyes to remove the marks of tears. Bethia was, I knew, aware that I was now a wife in truth, as Andrew had put it; henceforth she would expect me to behave like one, and I did what I could to gather the shreds of my dignity. What had been done was done, and there was no useful purpose in speaking of it; I knew that my will would not be considered in future. I had come home as mistress of Pless, it was true, but under orders from my husband.

He sent for me before dinner, to his study where he kept his accounts. Here everything was tidy, with the scrolls and ledgers balanced in neat piles or on the shelves Andrew had himself put up. It was as though he still lived in his log cabin, I thought scornfully; coming so fresh from Maverick, I could not contemplate the notion that any gentleman worked with his hands. I stood in silence, regarding this man who thought himself my master. His eyes looked back at me, blue in the clear light. I could guess that he had been out at his trees for most of the afternoon; he still wore his working clothes. Go whoring he might not, as Bethia had said, but the trees were my rival as much as any woman. The thought occurred to me while I waited for him to speak. He gestured me to a chair, and I sat down, arranging my skirts. The silence beat down between us for moments, and then he spoke.

"I must tell you, Primrose, of what occurred to bring me in such haste to Maverick."

"I have no wish to hear," I said coldly. He made an impatient movement, and went on. "Whether or not you wish to hear, hear you must. It is a matter that affects your good name, or could do if it went further. As far as I am concerned, it shall not."

He unfolded a piece of paper he had by him and cast it across the table-top to where I sat. I stared at it in unbelief: it was the Leda drawing. "A letter came with it," said Andrew. "It was unsigned."

"What did it say?" I said, forgetting my part in my bewilderment. Who could have made it their business to send Andrew such a drawing? It could hardly be Clun. Suddenly I thought of Lady Harry, and her smugness followed by her tears, and Havergal's report to me of the quarrel between husband and wife. If her ladyship had found the drawing in Clun's possession, and said nothing till she had sent it off to Andrew with the object of removing me from Maverick, then told Clun . . . it all fitted. I stared at the letter. It was brief, and said only *This is how your Wife spends her Days. Of her Nights I know nothing, but Some may.*

"It is not true," I said hotly. "My nights were spent as they should be, in my bed alone."

"I have ascertained that, as you know. But the truth about the drawing is less easily explained away. With whom were you so familiar as to expose yourself naked, and in such a pose?"

I looked at the drawing, which by now was hateful to me, with its spread legs and my face, recognisably portrayed, wearing the simpering expression of a Leda to whom the swan's embraces were not unwelcome. I blushed deeply, and wished the earth would swallow me. How must it appear to

Andrew that I had acted so, even if the artists were two harm-
less old ladies? I stammered out the truth, briefly. He nodded
and held out his hand for the drawing, which he tore in two
and then crumpled, throwing it in the fireplace. "I shall set a
light to that before I leave, so that no one, even a servant, may
find it," he said. "Fortunately I had heard of Leda as part of the
education you decry. I am glad that matters are clear between
us. I see that you could hardly have acted otherwise than you
did, on the invitation of such artists. In a way it is a pity that
the drawing must burn."

He rose and, kneeling by the grate, struck a tinder and burnt
the obnoxious thing, which writhed to thin ash. "I must tell
you for my part how matters sped," he said. "On receiving the
drawing and the note, I fell into a great rage, as you will
understand." He rose to his feet, dusted his hands and smiled.
"I went hotfoot to the Admiral, borrowed his coach, left word
here that you would be returning home with me, and hastened
to Maverick. When I arrived I was met by a footman, who by
great good chance had just conveyed a message to you to
repair to the summer-house, and so knew where you were.
Otherwise, from what I saw, it would have been too late to
rescue you. What madness made you encourage Clun? Even I
have heard of his excesses; he is a notorious rake, and no woman
of reputation will spend time in his company—certainly not
alone with him."

His voice was so stern that I began to weep. "Clun is
nothing to me," I said. "I gave him no encouragement. I was
lured to the summer-house by a message saying that you were
there, and I thought it strange, but went." Andrew had come
over and would have put his arms about me, but I jerked away.
"He plagued me during all my stay," I said, "and if you have
killed him, as you may have done, it doesn't matter to me, but
it will be more heard of with his being a lord."

"I doubt if he is dead, and such a lord is worth less than a
good farm-worker. Dry your tears, sweetheart. If Clun's path

and mine cross again it will be the worse for him, that is all; but I would have you a more cheerful bride."

I was thinking of several things; the thin length of Clun, the wiry tenacity of Andrew, so that it would be like a bulldog attacking a giraffe I had seen in a picture-book. I also thought of the footman, and the bewilderment he must have been in when he discovered that my husband was on the doorstep, not in the summer-house. I began to giggle suddenly; it was all of it too much.

Andrew had begun kissing me. "Then it is all forgotten, and from now on we live at Pless as man and wife, sharing all things." He stroked my neck.

"No," I said, my laughter suddenly gone. "No, I do not want it." I jumped from my chair and stalked to the window. Outside it had begun to rain, and the thrusting trees lifted their heads to the sky, as if to drink. I heard Andrew come over; from behind he laid his hands on my breasts. These were swollen and tender, I thought from his handling of last night, and I writhed away. He turned me round by the shoulders and I saw him frown. "Indeed," he said, "far from being the lightskirt I had thought you, Primrose, you act with me as though you were a nun. I can understand a young maid who fears for her maidenhead, but—" his face lightened and he smiled, the smile lighting up his eyes so that I dropped mine— "but you are a married woman now, and should have no more fear. What is it, sweetheart? Why are you afraid?"

But I turned away, for I would not tell him about Penuel. Instead I answered ungraciously "I did not ask for marriage. I mislike it, that is all. If you will oblige me, you will not touch me again; I want my bed to myself as I am used."

"Then you will have to learn otherwise," he said, "for my mind is set. I have been indulgent with you these many years, with little gratitude or affection in return; why, when that impudent miss you brought home with you was here, the pair of you often made me long to take a rod to your backs, but I controlled myself. Yet I am a man, and no monk; keep your nunlike airs if you will. I have told Bethia to prepare a room for us both. In future you shall sleep there with me; when your things come from Maverick, they will be moved there. Say no more, for I will not be persuaded. Go now, and make yourself ready for dinner."

I left him in my useless rage, which was only half fear; the other half was the thwarting of my will, for it was becoming evident that I could no longer prevail over my husband's. I was like a lost boat off course in a stormy sea, whose rudder is seized by someone who comes aboard, and makes it go where he will. I could see that the pattern of my life at Pless would be ordered by Andrew in the future, and that my carefree days were gone. Needless to say, I wept; the ladies of Maverick could have drawn me then as Niobe in truth. But they were far away, and I was here alone with my husband. I shuddered and thanked God that at least the Indian would not eat at our table tonight; he continued to prepare his own food for himself in the woods, which were his natural home.

## Twenty-two

THE TIME OF MY HONEYMOON, if that is what one must call it,
passed slowly enough with my fits of the sullens and Andrew's
efforts to lighten them, which proved useless. By the end he
treated me as I deserved to be treated. He was angry also that,
after all Miss Jule had taught me in the way of receipts and
household lore, I refused to cook for him. "It is not the habit
of polite persons to do such things," I informed him, adding that
I had no objection to instructing a cookmaid. Even this he
agreed to, and thereafter employed a willing young girl from
the farms, who in fact knew most of what I could teach her,
except for fancy touches. Had I applied myself to making
Pless a happy home for Andrew and for cooking him nourishing
meals, I might have raised the oppression which lay on my
spirits. As it was, I left the work to Bethia and the maid, lay
late in bed and thought of the delights I was missing at
Maverick. Andrew did not reproach me; by now he was busy
mixing a wash which would keep beetle and mould off his
trees. I heard of this from the servants. Andrew himself had
given up even the pretence that I might be interested in what he
was about, and spoke to me as seldom as possible. I hardly

saw him except when at nights he came to the bed we shared, and continued in his determination to make me a wife. I knew I was wretched, and never thought that he might be so also; it seemed to me that all a man demanded was bodily satisfaction, swiftly and without words or, these days, kisses. Had I even mocked at his grimly set face and stubborn manner it might have eased things between us so that they ended in laughter; but I thought myself hard done by, a martyr in fact, and either sulked with my face turned from him or wept, without result. Only one night I had rebelled and tried to refuse him his rights, struggling and clawing his face, and he imprisoned my hands and forced me to lie with him, hurting me no little. I heard him say in the darkness "Do your duty, or by God I will beat it into you." I was frightened, and after that let him do as he would, and little pleasure I must have given him.

One night it was different between us. I do not know whether Andrew had been gentler with me than of late, almost as he had been in the first days he brought me home, before I made an enemy of him. He was lying with me and for some reason I began to feel that I would like it if he stayed within me, and half aware of what I was doing curved my body to accommodate his the more readily. He said nothing, but as rarely now happened he kissed me, and fondled my body. I was beginning to feel a kind of languor steal through me, as if it were the prelude to some incomparable sweetness I had never known or thought of. What might have happened would have made all the difference to our fortunes, but suddenly with a kind of brusque shyness Andrew left me and turned over on his side to sleep. I lay awake for some time, feeling that I had been deprived of some experience I could not name. I wanted to touch Andrew and bring him back to me, but in my turn was shy.

Next morning as was his habit Andrew had risen and breakfasted before I was awake. I ate my own breakfast thoughtfully, filled with a strange desire that he should be seated opposite me, even in his despised shirt-sleeves and with the sunlight glinting on his hair. I did not yet know what it was I wanted to say to him, only that I would like to be near him if I could. With this curious purpose in mind I stole out after I had breakfasted and made my way to the thick woods.

The trees were huge. In the state I was for once in I could think of Andrew instead of myself and it came to me that he had worked long and hard for many years to achieve this result. His toil would soon repay itself; the trees stood in their radial rows tall, healthy and straight. They had a height no ordinary tree could boast, though I had not then heard of the giant redwoods of America. Their shadows were so long that each tree, in the morning sun, shaded its neighbour well up the trunk, so that their dun hues mingled with sharply angled shadows. For the first time in my life the greatness of the attempt to grow these trees was borne in upon me and, perhaps, I saw behind the dogged blunt exterior of the person who was Andrew and could begin, only begin to see the vision which inspired his purpose and hard work. Here was a dream, transformed to living reality. I stretched out a hand and almost timidly stroked the smooth bark, as though it were a human limb. Then I went on my way somewhat aimlessly. I had no idea in which part of the wood Andrew would be, or even what I should say to him when we met. All I knew was that for a little while I wanted to watch him without his seeing me, to reassure myself of something, though I was uncertain what it was. I walked on between the dazzle of early sun and the sharp shadows and thrusting sentinels of trees. At the centre of the wood, if I must reach it, one could see down every avenue and find out where Andrew was; but I hoped to find him before having to go near where the Indian lived.

A shout brought Andrew to my notice; he was giving orders about the disposal of barrows of peat, heaped darkly nearby the central hut. He turned, without seeing me, and

walked over and began to examine a tree. I saw his strong
hands run over the bark, not as mine had done but know-
ledgeably, almost as though he caressed a woman, almost as
he might, if I gave him fair reason, handle me, perhaps
tonight, if. . . . The blood rushed into my face; I stood there
looking at Andrew with my thoughts in chaos, not knowing
what to say or do.

I was observed: I should have known it. After a time
watching Andrew examine the tree, and its neighbour, something made me turn. A little way off stood the Indian, leaning
against a tree-trunk and regarding me. The expression in his
eyes was a mixture of contempt, certain knowledge, and a
quality without name. I felt soiled; I turned and ran. It did not
occur to me that Saginaw would tell Andrew that I, his wife,
had been in the wood watching him; I knew he would not
mention me. I ran till my breath came in sobbing gasps, got
myself home and to a place where none saw me. I still felt
ashamed, as if I had shown myself naked.

That night Andrew came to me as usual and I was cold
with him, as was my former custom. I sensed a certain disappointment in him, as if he had been led to expect better
things. Whatever they were, I downed the thought of them and
put them from me, and presently put Andrew from me also,
and we turned our separate ways to sleep without further
words.

What happened next made an end of any likelihood there
might have been that Andrew and I would after all deal
lovingly together as husband and wife.

It happened the day after my expedition to the wood. I
woke feeling queasy, and could not face my morning chocolate
when Bethia brought it. She looked at me with a knowing eye.
Later she came back. I was better, but wanted no breakfast,
and told her so. "I expect I chilled myself yesterday, going
out early," I said vaguely. My whole body felt different, as

if I no longer possessed myself; when I sat up, my head swam. I saw the old servant nodding wisely.

"That's no chill," she said, and showed her worn teeth in a grin. "That's childer. You be with bairn, ma'am." She turned to pick up the chocolate tray and I thrust it aside with so fierce a kick that it overturned and spilled on the carpet, making a muddy pool and a clatter of pewter.

I screamed. "No! No! No! It isn't true . . . it can't be. I won't have it, I won't." And Bethia laughed. "Ye'll needs have it, for it's there. Not to show yet, though. Bide a while, in your bed, then get up for y'dinner." But I lay and yelled and drummed on the bed with my feet, and worked myself into so alarming a state that the servants took fright, and spoke of sending for Mr. Andrew. The thought of my husband was the last straw. In my mind was the horror of a back-street slum behind the Canongate of Edinburgh, and a bloody dish and the thing lying in it, that went down the privy.

"No! No!" I screamed. "I never want to see him again. Take him away. I never want to see . . . never . . . never . . .".

Someone turned then and went out. Later I learned that Andrew had been there. He had come straight to me, pleased with the news they brought him, and would have taken me in his arms in front of them all. Now I had killed whatever spark of kindness he still felt for me; I had shamed him, made him look a fool; I saw it for myself. That night he did not come to my bed, nor on any night thereafter.

## Twenty-three

ONE WEAPON had always remained with me; I had been pretty, and could get my way often with a twist of the waist or a flutter of eyelashes, or the turning away of a rose-petal cheek. Now I lost my looks, and was accordingly in a state of helpless bewilderment and rage. After some weeks the sickness I had begun to feel in the mornings stopped, but soon I began to thicken. I still thought of the coming child with loathing and dread. Once at the beginning I made a posset of herbs to try to do away with it. Bethia caught me at it, however, and it was one of the rare times when I have seen her angry and when she forgot that she was a servant and I her mistress. "Ye have a good man and treat him like the dirt beneath y'feet," she said, her hairy face flushed and her hands squared into great fists, as if for Andrew's protection. "Destroy his child? Not while I have breath and tongue," and she took the caudle of herbs and cast it on the fire, where it hissed and steamed. I had my customary resort to tears. "Ay, cry, do," said Bethia. "Self-love ye have in plenty, but mortal pity for another, even your own man and bairn? Not a whit, that I can see," and she herded me off to my chamber where I now slept alone, to lie down till I should have recovered from the effects of excitement and her scolding. I know she mentioned the matter to Andrew, because he became strict and watchful, seldom now leaving me to my own devices but always making certain that one of the servants should be within sight, if he were absent. As always, he spent most of his time at the plantings; the trees now gained in height so fast one could almost see them growing, and I heard him say the queen-tree had darkened in colour and the seed-box was almost as large as it would become. I compared myself bitterly and unreasonably to this queen, my rival. I believe Andrew's mind was occupied so much that it enabled him to be patient with me as of no relative importance. Otherwise I must have driven him mad.

I had swelled almost to pear-shape when the invitation came for Mary Cantlie's wedding. She was to marry a landowner somewhat to the east, near enough to Pless for frequent visiting. The bridegroom was of good family, which would please Mary, but had no money to speak of. I assumed it was a love-match and that the good Duchess had provided Mary with a dowry. I longed to go—it would be the first diversion I had had since Maverick, and I wanted to hear from Mary about her London season, and how many other proposals she had had, and the like. Yet I shrank from appearing in my ungainly state. "Soon I won't be able to see my own feet," I grumbled to Bethia. "And as for gowns, what am I to wear? Nothing I ever had for company will fit me now," and I began to cry, which I did as frequently nowadays as if I contained a lake of tears. Bethia said nothing and went over to the clothes-chest, then announced calmly, "The old watered satin will do, for there's a fall of lace will hide y'waist, and we can latch it loose."

"Waist? I have none left," I grumbled, but let her try on the watered satin, which was the one Miss Jule had made for me to go to Maverick. I had worn it once or twice there and sighed at having to be seen again in the same gown; but it would be enough to obtain Andrew's permission to go to the wedding at all, I thought, without asking him for new clothes into the bargain. How long ago Maverick seemed, or the sight of a friendly face! If it occurred to me that my situation was partly my own fault, I downed the thought promptly. Everything was Andrew's doing, from being doggedly busy with his trees, sparing no time for his wife—I did not think of the injustice of this when I had made it plain I did not wish for his company—and there was only Bethia who nowadays scolded always, and Saginaw of dark memories; no one else. I admitted grudgingly that I might as well wear the watered satin, as I looked a fright in any case; and marched off to tell Andrew I much desired to go and see Mary married.

To my surprise he made no difficulty, and even offered to ride over to the Admiral's and ask him again to lend his carriage, for my comfort on the journey. After he had ridden off I reflected that the last time I had sat in it, weeping, had been after my wedding-night. Andrew returned well pleased with the loan, over which the Admiral had made no difficulty, and the wine he had swallowed on the visit.

"It is good of him to lend the coach," he said. "Although he has small patience with fools he is none so bad a man. He says he will put in a word with the Admiralty for early inspection of the trees, with regard to a contract for wood for tall masts." I shrugged; the Admiral and my father had never dealt together, but then no one did deal with father.

The day came and I was carefully laced into the watered satin, and looked like a foaling mare. Bethia went and got out a white embroidered shawl with fringes, which had belonged to my mother.

"That will hide all of doomsday," she said, and draped the shawl over my shoulders, I knew I could make graceful play with it and it relieved my mind somewhat. Afterwards, in the coach, I was alone on the well-sprung cushions, for Andrew had elected to ride outside, no doubt so that he need not put up with my tongue. Looking back I can see what a shrew and scold I must have been, and marvel at his patience. By the time we had travelled to the church where Mary was to be married I was tired, for it was some hours since we had stopped at an inn for refreshment. I smiled, however; I must not cast a gloom on the wedding-ceremony. Andrew gave me his arm in punctilious fashion and we walked together down the aisle like any married couple, and were shown to a pew. The church was already full of company in feathered hats and turbans and rustling silks, so that it was difficult to see the bride when she appeared. I could see the groom, however, for he was as tall as my long-ago descriptions of Andrew to the Lawnmarket young ladies. He had a long humourless face and was not handsome; it must be his name that made him eligible.

At the feasting afterwards I ate but little, and afterwards, when the dancing was to start, retired to a place by the wall where Andrew found me a chair. He would have remained by me, but I told him to go away. I must often have hurt Andrew's feelings, though he never showed it. It is ironical that the expense of the education he had paid for had made me ashamed of him in front of my high-bred friends. I sat alone, for I do not know where he went to and he did not dance.

I tried to divert myself by watching the company, circling about the floor. Mary wore an ivory gown and a French veil which had belonged to her mother. She had taken several turns about the floor with her long groom when the pair came over to speak to me. Shortly after that a new arrival came in; someone I had never expected to see so deep in our country, and the sight of him gave me so little pleasure that I wished Andrew were again by my side. It was none other than Lord Harry Clun, whom I had last seen stretched out unconscious on the floor of Maverick summer-house. In no time at all, after he had greeted the married pair, his eyes found me. The expression in them was as wild as ever, and he made straight for my chair.

I was distressed; I did not know whether to pray that

Andrew might return, or that he might not. It was hardly possible that there should not be trouble between the two men if they met. Clun had seated himself by me, and straightway embarked upon the kind of flirtation which had ended so disastrously at Maverick. I was angry. "Can you not judge my state?" I said. "Have some regard for it, I pray you." I wished he would take himself off to some other female, but he showed no signs of doing so.

"You manage your shawl so beautifully that I had not at first guessed it," he said, "but in any case it makes you even more desirable. You are Ceres now, now Leda."

"I wonder that you dare remind me of that," I said. He made a grimace, and said "The matter was taken out of my hands, as you know. Had you heard of your cousin Thornton's engagement? The fair Augusta has succumbed."

I had not heard, and wished Thornton good luck of his heiress; her fortune would certainly repair his. I asked Clun to wish them happy, and had no doubt that I would be informed by letter when either of them had time to write. I encouraged Clun to give me more news; anything was preferable to sitting with his hot breath on my cheek and his eyes devouring me.

He obliged, telling me that when I had left him he had, on coming to himself, been desolate and with a damned sore jaw; there had been no more gaiety at Maverick after I had gone. Even the water-party had been called off as it had rained, and all the Chinese lanthorns on the island were ruined. I let him talk on gladly, taking consolation in the fact that I had after all missed very little gaiety. When Clun minded his manners, he could be diverting, and despite everything I was pleased with him for so lightly dismissing his defeat in the summer-house and for his continued homage to myself. We talked together for perhaps a quarter of an hour before I perceived the figure of my husband, making his determined way through the throng, and at last bowing stiffly before us. Hastily, I decided that the only thing to do was to present Clun; after all, he had behaved well and perhaps Andrew would do the same. But the latter looked ominous, and I hastened to make the introduction before worse befell.

"This is my husband Andrew Farquharson, whose abiding passion is his trees." Clun had risen and both men bowed, but in no friendly fashion; then I heard Clun say "I cannot conceive why they are his *chief* passion; perhaps they are not."

Later, as he handed me into the waiting carriage, Andrew scolded me. "You might show discretion when making these observations to strangers," he said, and I could tell that he was much displeased, though it seemed to me the fault was not great.

I shrugged. "Why should I? Half the world knows that trees grow at Pless."

"The less they know and try to conjecture the better," was all he would say then. But later when we were back at Pless he returned to the theme.

"Are you not aware," he said, "that I have spent these many years, and Saginaw also, in the constant care of the trees, in order that they may be the first to grow in the country, that we and no one else may reap the reward? Now you go and throw the matter wide open to a fool like Clun, who may misuse what he knows if only out of spite."

"He is unlikely to trouble," I said crossly. "He is of the great world, and has more to do than spend all day digging trenches and carting peat."

"I don't doubt that," said Andrew drily, and rose and went out to his study, closing the door after him. I felt chilled and miserable, and half sorry that we had gone to Mary's wedding at all. But it would perhaps be pleasant to have her within occasional visiting-distance.

The next wedding was Thornton's. It took place in Yorkshire, at the bride's home. They had not yet decided on an establishment of their own, and would spend some time in looking at houses afterwards. In the letter that came with our invitation Thornton stated that he had sold his commission which Andrew had purchased long ago, and was now, one presumed, a country gentleman of anticipated means. There was no offer of returning the money to Andrew. My husband had certainly received short shrift in his dealings with our family.

Although we had been bidden to the wedding, I could not this time face the journey, even in the Admiral's coach; I was grown very big. I spent my days idling, no longer making even a pretence to direct the maids; this I left to Bethia, who had gradually raised herself from servant to acting companion. No doubt I needed one, but I still liked to go off for walks by myself if I could, as in the days with Miss Minney and Miss Jule. As the time passed and my girth increased, the walks became shorter. Mary, making a courtesy-call, laughed at me. "Wait till you see it, and then you will be fond of it and feel that all the trouble was worth while," she said, with some wistfulness as her lanky bridegroom had not proved so adequate as yet. I closed my eyes and hid my distaste at the thought that I would ever grow fond of my child. A nurse could care for it, for I would not. I might not even survive the birth.

# Twenty-four

A RESTLESSNESS came upon me as the time of the birth drew near; it was of little help that nobody, myself least of all, knew the exact date of it. I was so big by now that surely it must happen soon; and it was pure mischance that one day Andrew looked at me, with a compassion which made me cross, and said "Do not walk as far as you have been doing, Primrose. You must save your strength, and how would you fare if the child came suddenly, when you were far from help?"

Although I had felt languid that day and had in fact made up my mind not to go for a walk, I decided now, to spite him, that I would walk to the furthest part of the planting, skirting the trees on my way in case I met Andrew himself or Saginaw. The latter had almost ceased to be a part of our lives, working steadily through the seasons when the trees needed attention; at the resting periods, which I knew were twice a year, he was off to seek diversion and women, leaving Andrew to guard the trees alone. I had heard of the Indian's being seen as far away as the Cumbrian horse-fairs. My newsvendor had been Mary, who still regarded Saginaw with open horror as a major item of gossip in her dull life. Yes, Mary now was dull; her marriage

had early proved a disappointment, and she wrote to me
frequently to while away the time.

Thinking of her, I scrambled my way among the rough
outer growth of willow-herb and teazle which had been allowed
to come up beyond the pruned outer ring of trees. There had
been a stony path here when I was a child, but it was so little
used that it was by now hardly a track, as I had not realised
before I came today. I felt the heads of teazle pull at me and
remembered how Penuel used to pick them and turn them
about in her long fingers and tell me that animals and people
carried them far from the place of growth on their clothes and
fur, thus spreading the plant over wide spaces. They clung now
to my skirts with their hooks, and I did not pick them off.
Soon I would come to the marshland remaining beyond the
plantings and there I could stride out as I would, spreading
teazles in the wild or doing as I wished. I felt myself a part of
nature today, half forgetting the child I carried within me
which made my breath labour. How thankful I should be to
be rid of its weight! This was small wonder, I told myself; I
had been forced to conceive. It was a bitter thought for a girl
of seventeen.

It was while I was still toiling up the erstwhile path that the
pains took me. At first they were only short, sharp reminders
in the small of my back, and when they started I turned, biting
my lip in vexation that Andrew should have been right, and
I should not have come on so long a walk. I would get back in
time, I swore. This was earlier than the expected birth-date as
Bethia had worked it out, and later than I had; perhaps I was
going to miscarry. Despite my fear, a strange uplifting feeling
filled me, half curiosity, half relief. It was as though I watched
myself from somewhere else, and could ignore the pains.

But they were becoming too strong to be ignored, and as time
went by I had to admit to myself that I might not reach Pless.
The thought of giving birth to a child in the open, like a
gypsy, scared me; I told myself that it was impossible that this

should happen to me, Primrose Farquharson; then I thought how much better it would be had I been a gypsy indeed, for they have knowledge which helps them in such case. I was hurrying, almost running, when a bramble-arch caught my foot and I fell, landing on my hands and knees. I got myself up, more frightened than hurt, but the fall had hurried on the birth-pains and soon I felt a wetness between my thighs. The child was coming. I waited for it to happen, then, as nothing did, I went on, hearing the sound of my muffled, dragging, frightened footsteps among the high weeds. Andrew had been right; if I could reach Andrew . . . I cried out, and heard the echoes of my voice.

Steady, regular pains had begun again; different from the first, more urgent, as though another will were already forcing itself on mine. I struggled on; the nearest shelter was the hut in the wood, and loathing the thought as I did I made for it, hoping at least that Saginaw would be out, at the trees. Perhaps also I might find Andrew near the centre, or at least see where he was if I could still see anything. The sweat was coursing down my face in runnels, making my eyes blind. "Someone will go for help," I said repeatedly against the grinding, implacable pain. I made towards the trees.

Never had I had more cause to bless the radial paths than now. Between the giant sentinels I hurried, hearing my own breaths sound like the tearing of cloth. I bit my lip to prevent myself from howling with the pain; the Indian must not see me so. If the hut were nearer. . . .

I saw it then, through the branches. I stumbled towards it, feeling a swift agony which was worse than any I had undergone before. The child's head was being born. I gathered my skirts, still dragging on, feeling the half-born creature try to free itself from me. Could I in fact give birth walking? Here was the door from which long ago I had been shut out while the Indian took Penuel within, on the bed of birch. Now it was open. Thank God, there was someone inside. I cried aloud. There was the slow bright fire, where the Indian cooked his food. There would be some water.

I lurched into the hut, past Saginaw's dark form, and dropped Alexander Farquharson on the trodden floor of earth. By then I was on my knees, groaning and crying. I had forgotten who heard me or whether or not I cared that they should, and who I was, and whose child I had borne. I was glad of the shelter and warmth and remember nothing more than sinking into a state that was half sleep, half unconsciousness.

When I came to myself the Indian was no longer in the hut. Someone had lifted me on to the birch bed and its springy strength supported my back. I was alone except for the little bloodstained animal that lay by me, mewling weakly. The pains still ground in me, but less strongly. Saginaw must have laid the baby by me, and gone for help. I would not stay on the bed where he had taken Penuel. I turned and rolled over, getting myself off the brushwood and on to the floor. Then I started to crawl. I would not stay in the hut. Somehow I found the door and got myself through it, then I was writhing, weak and slow, along the path that led back to Pless. To keep enough strength to get myself out of the forest before I died . . . to see the bright day. . . .

I remember lifting my head to stare along the pitiless corridor of giants, and collapsing on to the carpet of last year's leaves.

They came then and carried me back to Pless, and it was there that the second twin, also a boy, was born, but of that I remember little.

I do not know how long I slept. I awoke to my own room and a fire and Bethia bending over the wooden cradle in which I myself had been born, crooning to her two beauties. Two! That would account for my girth, and for the unexpected onset of the pains. I wanted to talk, but not to Bethia. However I called her and she came over, and laid a large placid hand on my forehead. "Awake, then, my love? A fine fright ye gave 'em. Poor Mr. Andrew and the Injun came, and carried you and all of it home, and praise God no harm done that we can see. Two fine boys, Mrs. Primrose; 'twere well done, but for the place of't. The master told ye not to go out walking, and go ye would."

She brought me a posset to drink. "There, that brings back strength. In no time at all ye'll be sitting up, and have the dears by ye one on each side. Shall I bring them now, for ye to take a peep?"

I turned my head away. I did not want to see the two little animals. I supposed Saginaw had told Andrew about the one I had left in the hut, lying on the birch pallet. It was like a cat littering. I was too tired to think further, or even to wonder why Andrew was not by me.

Later I found that Andrew was very angry, almost as much so as he had been the time he came and fetched me back from Maverick. As soon as I was well enough to sit up he came to me. "Do not expect me to congratulate you," he said grimly.

"I expect nothing. I am not a tree."

"You left that poor baby in the hut, where he might have died had Saginaw not seen the birth and told me where to find him. Why could you not at least have waited quietly till help came? The first act was foolish disobedience, the second downright wickedness."

"I did not know that there was to be a second birth, nor did anyone." I closed my eyes; evidently he saw that he was tiring me, and I heard him rise from the bedside where he sat.

"You knew and cared nothing. It is by the mercy of Providence that both my sons are alive and well. They have had little help into this world from their mother."

I thought of the travail I had endured, and tears of self-pity trickled from under my eyelids. Sounds of sucking from beyond the near door told me that the children had been found a wet-nurse. I was glad not to have to feed them myself, for, as I told myself, Andrew in his present mood might have expected anything of me, and I could hardly bear to have them touch me. I spoke aloud in case he was still in the room.

"As I am of so little help," I said, "permit me to move back to the tower wing where I used to sleep, and the nurse may come in here with the children and you will have them and Providence for company."

"You may do as pleases you best; you do so in any case," he said angrily, and went out. I called Bethia and gave orders that my things were to be moved back to my old room near the apple-tree. She murmured, and I snapped at her to mind her own affairs.

On my moving out, I took a heedless glance at the children in their cradle. To my surprise, they looked less revolting than I had expected: they had lost the blueness of birth and the blood had all been washed away, and they were growing a fluff of hair on their heads. Alexander's—his name had been settled some time before—was red as a carrot, James's dark like my own. But I would not come down from my high solitary place and show affection for them now. I had been told that I was unhelpful; I should remain so. And it was as certain as the sky above me, I decided, that I would bear no more children to Andrew or any man.

# Twenty-five

THE DAY-TO-DAY LIFE of a selfish young woman makes dull
hearing. All of that year I walked, rode, did as I pleased, as
Andrew had said; sometimes from my tower I would catch a
glimpse of my children, less often of their father, who was
frequently away on his overseeing of the beaver merchandise
at the auctions in London. I understood that this part of his
business was thriving; it made itself felt in little luxuries,
horses in the stable, a carriage if I wished to use it (I seldom did),
and more servants, besides the dry-nurse who had come to
look after the children and who stayed on, and would do till
they required a tutor.

The children sat up, then crawled, then began to stagger
on their feet; Jamie was slower than Alicky, who had evidently
resolved to continue in his precipitate behaviour on entering
this world. Sometimes, when their father was absent, I would
go to try to make them know me, and tempt them with fruit or
kisses; but they were shy with me, and would run and bury
their heads in the nurse's skirts, or Bethia's. After a time I
accepted this; after all, it had been what I wanted.

Now and again Mary drove over, or I would ride to visit

her. This was almost my only diversion, and Clun had not been in the neighbourhood again. Mary had discontinued her house-parties and most forms of entertainment by the time she had been married a year. "I declare I wish I had never come here, the company is so dull," she complained, yawning one day when I had ridden over, on the cushions of the day-sofa she affected, as if she had been an invalid. I looked at her sallow face, pinched with discontent and unhealthy with too much staying indoors, and by contrast felt myself fit with the ride in the morning breezes and bright air. Percy, the husband, was nowhere to be seen. I believe he always slept very late after a night with the port. There were still no children.

As if I had mentioned him, Mary did so. "He is with the lawyers, to see if they can settle an asking-price for the house."

"You have decided to sell already?" I was surprised, but did not mourn much. Mary was no longer her lively self, and Percy made so poor a showing as a country gentleman that he could hardly sit a horse. "Yes, indeed," she said. "I pine for the town; I should never have left it."

"Yet you did so knowing that Percy's forebears had lived here for generations."

The sloe-dark eyes surveyed me. "We do not always act as we have intended," she said. "Have your own fortunes turned out as you foresaw? Yet you are lucky; Andrew they say is becoming a rich man. When the trees are sold, you will be able to buy anything in this world."

Except love, I thought. I felt sorry for Mary, and for her lack-lustre husband, and even sorrier for myself. We parted with affectionate exchanges, but truth to tell were no longer friends. I rode home at breakneck speed, as if to shake off the stale air of Mallet Grange.

I wondered about the house. If it were in fact for sale, it might suit Thornton and his Augusta, who had not yet found themselves a suitable home. Whether it would be pleasant to have them near I did not consider; nor did I envisage other things which might happen if they became neighbours. This is true, and shows a lack of guile in me. However on reaching Pless I was met by news which put all thoughts of Mallet, Thornton and Mary out of my head, and caused me to pack my gear for a journey at once. Miss Minney had died. The news had come while I was out.

I thought of little Miss Jule, left alone in the long white cottage, and set off in my carriage, the better to bring her to Pless. She could not continue alone, and although Andrew was away at present, I knew he would be pleased to offer her a home.

When the house came in sight I alighted and went in at once, to comfort her. She was sitting alone, by a fire which burned brightly from habit, as though she had made herself do all those things she did daily, but now they were finished. She shed no tears. Had Miss Minney been the one who was left, there would have been much weeping and wailing. I tried to tell Miss Jule how fortunate it was that she, the stronger, was left. "She could never have contrived without you," I said again and again. I doubted if Miss Minney could even have fed herself; for so many years she had sat, like the large chick to which I had formerly compared her, having food brought to her and all her needs met. In the end, it had been a condition of the heart that carried her off; I heard all this later from the physician.

Miss Jule might not have heard me; she continued to stare into the fire. I thought of the large family there had been, all of whom she had nursed till they died. Now she said "Nobody needs me any more," and fell silent.

"I need you. You will be welcome at Pless." But she would not agree to come. At one time she roused herself enough to realise who I was and said "Ye have your man and weans; ye'll not need me," but that was the only time she spoke of Pless. She would not leave her house, and sat waiting for I know not what, except that it must be death. I tried to persuade her to eat, to take a dish of tea, a glass of her own home-made wine, but it was useless. She did not even bid me eat after my journey; in the end, being very hungry, I stole a bite of food in a corner. It was clear that my presence made no difference to her: no more, I told myself sadly, than it made to my own family at Pless.

I tried again. "The children will love you," I said. I told her of the boys, how they were running about and strong, and then remembered her only brother, who had died at twenty. No matter what I said it seemed to hinge on sadness; so in the end I fell as silent as she, and we sat one on each side of the fire.

I stayed on at the cottage, for I could not leave her as she was. She had always kept close to herself, encouraging no neighbours; no one had mattered, by the end, except Miss Minney. What was to happen now? Every now and again I would hear again in my mind the sad words. "No one needs me." I began to apply them to myself.

The days passed, and I had sent the carriage home. I wondered what was happening at Pless and if Andrew had returned. I believed that he would not have done so yet: it was some time since he had been south, and there would be much business to transact. "Perhaps also he keeps a woman," I thought, though there had never been any sign of this. I remembered his words to me that he was not a monk, though he had been patient. I remembered many things.

Nine days after Miss Minney's death, Miss Jule died. The cause of her death was the same heart condition. The tale sounds unlikely, but that was the truth; I had watched her daily wish herself into her grave. Perhaps a broken heart can be described in this way, for she had died of grief.

When the will was read I learnt that Miss Jule had left her small possessions to me, having no blood-relatives left. I brought the items carefully home to Pless; the pancake-girdle, the polished brass jelly-pan, a candlestick with snuffers and bell, other such things. I kept them all in my own room at Pless and would not allow them to be used in the kitchen, and I cleaned them myself. Now and again I would look at them and think of Miss Jule, and her life and its end. Generally after such thoughts I would have a mount saddled and ride out. I no longer went to see Mary at her house; there was small comfort from that quarter.

One day, as I had meant to do before I left, I sat down and wrote a letter to Thornton. To have him and the former Miss Desmond near Pless would be a change, at the least. Besides, I knew that they wanted a place to live and Mallet Grange would shortly be on the market, and they might conclude an advantageous deal if they made their offer first. Would I have written the letter had I known what the final purchase would bring to us all at Pless? Perhaps I would not; and yet again perhaps I would.

Thornton, or rather Augusta, did buy Mallet, and Mary and Percy moved to a house in town where I hope they are more contented. The Milhalls moved in before the end of the year. It was odd to have Thornton close again.

## Twenty-six

As I HAVE STATED, I had not thought that Thornton and Augusta's purchase of Mallet Grange would mean the re-entry into my life of Harry Clun. How should I? When I had first met with him at Maverick he and my cousin were on an amiable, but hardly close footing; and the next time I had seen him was at Mary's wedding, and Mary now was gone. What I did not know was that birds of a feather indeed flock together; over the years the acquaintance of Clun with Thornton had ripened, mostly over the gaming-tables. Clun was now a near enough friend of Thornton's to accept frequent invitations to Mallet, or even, as I became swiftly aware, to invite himself. I learned later that he diverted Augusta, who God knows was in need of diversion, for Thornton neglected her now she was in an interesting situation. As for Lady Harry, she never came north.

Again as I have said, I used to ride out frequently in the mornings. There were few ways outside the forest for a shod horse to follow, and generally I would ride along the track where my disastrous walk the day of the births had taken me. Andrew had had it cleared and smoothed with sand and sawdust to make a bridle-path, and now it was wide and firm, with the brambles well cut back and burned at the root. One fine day I let my mount amble and turned my eyes to the charred patches where traces of curled new bracken showed green, for it survives even fire. When I looked up it was to see a horseman rein in, sweeping off his hat with an exaggerated gesture. It was Clun.

"Mrs. Farquharson—ma'am—a good day." He was no whit perturbed that he was on Andrew's land; there was no end to the man's insolence. I slewed round my mare's head, and made to ride back, turning to ask over my shoulder "What is your business here?" For I knew he was trespassing whether or not he did so.

"Why, I am staying at Mallet, and rode out early and far in the very hope of seeing so fair a vision as yourself. Do not leave me when we have only just met; cannot we be friends?" He stretched out a hand and tried to capture my reins, but I whisked them away from him. "You should have thought of friendship earlier," I said, and cantered off on Rosemary, who like many a dappled mare had quick wits.

A person of less effrontery than Clun would not have appeared on the bridle-path again, but he did so, and his conversation, or such as I allowed him, always took a gallant turn, which made me impatient. I tried the few other ways there were, but Clun found out and followed me to each one of them. In the end, I gave up riding. This angered me, for I had enjoyed it and it had taken my thoughts from myself; also, it was dull by contrast to have to walk close to the house. However I did not think even Clun would penetrate there. He must know only too well what Andrew thought of him, even though they had met on that one occasion since my husband's uppercut to Clun's jaw in the summer-house at Maverick. If they were to meet again, especially were I to complain to Andrew of having been followed on my rides, I did not doubt the outcome; it might be, this time, swords or pistols, though I knew Clun to be such a coward that he avoided duelling at any cost. So I said nothing of it all, the few times I saw my husband nowadays.

Other things troubled me, and they were nothing to do with Clun.

I had come in from my walk one day, pulling off my hat and gloves and moving to my window, meaning to open it because of the heat. When I put my hand to the latch and leaned out it was to see Andrew, with the children and their nurse who had just come out, below on the grass. He was playing with the twins, who whooped with delight; I saw Andrew toss Jamie up in his arms again and catch him, and the child's glee. I was unaccustomed to see high spirits in the boys, for I think the nurse had warned them to be on their best behaviour with their mother. For their father, evidently— I drew a long breath—it was different. I did not envy him the twins' love, I realised now; I envied them his.

I stared down in that long moment. I remember the sun catching Andrew's smooth hair, and as though they were not even familiar to me saw, but in an entirely new way, the features that made him what he was. The determined jaw was there, the muscular shoulders grown broad with digging, the set of the way he stood, as though challenging the world, but quietly. How many hundred times had I seen him thus, and taken no notice? Yet in this moment I knew he filled all of my life. How long had I loved him? I could not tell; perhaps longer than the children, but I had been shut away for too long in my own secret places of pride and bitter memory and self-love to be certain. I turned back into the room, dazedly determined not to torment myself further; if he caught sight of me at the window, what more would he give me than a cool good-day?

That night I lay broad awake, tossing on my bed. It was as though every horizon of my life had shifted and also as if I had shed a skin, as a caterpillar will. I could feel hurt pricking at the new skin, and new awareness in my body and in my mind.

Love is not always sudden; mine must have grown, in sight of Andrew's kindness and patience, for a long time. But he would never forgive me for my early coldness, I was convinced, still less for my behaviour at the time of the boys' birth. If he had ever had a brief fondness for me he had lost it long ago; and I had nobody to blame but myself.

I got up and went to my clothes-chest and at length found the beaver muff Andrew had sent me years since in the Lawn-market, resting my hot cheek against the silky fur. I had lost him, I knew; too many things stood between us, and I could never, while his blood-brother still worked by his side in the forest, say what had happened between Penuel and Saginaw, and what it had done to me.

## Twenty-seven

THE TREES BEGAN their final spurt of growth and once again they oppressed me. I knew Andrew was well pleased with them and was beginning to send out enquiries to shipping firms and, on our neighbour's suggestion, even the Admiralty. I tried to feel gladness for his sake that his life's work—it was hardly less—had ended, or would soon do so, in triumph and riches. But I was sick at heart and at times felt that if I could not win out of the encircling trees, I would pine away like a plant which cannot breathe or reach the sun.

In this mood I wrote to Mary, from whom I had not heard since she settled herself and Percy in a small house in London. There was nothing particular about my letter except that it made clear the fact that I was grown somewhat weary of country existence, as she herself had been. No reply came and I told myself bitterly that Mary had too many diversions now to write. No doubt her time was taken up with balls, routs, and assemblies; it was the life she wanted and I sought to be glad for her sake that it had been contrived in whatever manner; the sale of Mallet would have brought them in some money.

Meantime a further episode had vexed me at Pless. One

day I was walking in the grounds, idly, my mind empty even of my love for Andrew, for there was no purpose in brooding on that. He continued courteous, no more. We seldom saw each other except at meals, and then he was not always present. I knew he sometimes went down and shared a game-stew with the Indian, or again, in his rare times of leisure, he might be invited over to the Admiral's to shoot. The Admiral did not exchange visits any more than he ever had, and never came to dine at Pless. In my morbid state I told myself it was because the old man disliked me. It is more probable that, his long-dead spouse having been a fool, he had decided to rid his life of all women. However he liked Andrew's company and they had many a good day on the marshes and moors.

As I walked now, there came the sound of tapping. It was unmistakeably tapping on wood and I heard it now here, now there among the trees. Later it stopped, and I returned to the house and passed the day as usual; Andrew was not in for dinner and I ate mine in solitude, then went to bed.

Next day I saw him at breakfast. He seemed to be in a state of suppressed excitement, which could not be controlled even at sight of me. His blue eyes sparkled and he seemed filled with a joy which had left him, perhaps, since as a lad he took ship for Canada and left his family. I handed him his coffee and he said "Primrose, there is talk of an Admiralty tender. Some experts—oh, an engineer, a chemist, and the like—were here yesterday, and inspected the trees. Their hopes were surpassed; they had not believed my letter. The trees they say are of a height and strength to make superb masts for ships of the line, and such things; meantime, it must be confirmed from London."

"You did not bring them here to dine," I told him. He looked up from his plate and a brief expression I could not name passed over his face, then was gone. "No, I took them to the inn; we had business to discuss," he answered briefly.

I said nothing, concealing my hurt. Was I so little a part of

Andrew's life that he had not thought to bring his guests home, as the inn was more companionable? I managed to smile and said "When there are other visitors, bring them here. There is no need to go to the expense of inn-meals."

"We shall soon be rich," he said gaily. "However, when my lords of the Admiralty come to see the forest, you shall play hostess to them. Get out your cookery-lore from Miss Jule; you seldom use it."

It was true; from idleness, I seldom did, and Bethia and the young farm-girl still saw to most of our meals. I was suddenly ashamed. "I will try to use it before then," I told him, "but you are sometimes not at home for dinner. Inform me, pray, when you will be in, and I will show my talents."

"Well done," he said lightly, and went out to his trees. I watched him go, clenching my fists to hide my rising temper. He cared nothing for me, nothing! I might as well have become Clun's mistress: were I to do so it would not disturb Andrew one whit.

That day I saddled the dappled mare again, and rode out careless of whether or not I should meet Clun, or anyone. I rode as far as Thornton's house and saw Augusta, who was alone; neither Thornton nor Clun were staying at Mallet. "All we women are abandoned, I suppose," I told her, shrugging. The watery eyes raised themselves and Augusta said "Indeed, yes," without any humour. I left her in a worse temper than when I had ridden in; how dull she was! Well, she had been married for her money, I for my land; what use to repine?

Next day a long letter sealed in red, and a crest of a couching greyhound, came for me. I opened it and in astonishment saw that it was from the Duchess at Maverick. She had seen Mary in town, and had heard that I was weary of my life; would I come and visit her? "*I had it in mind to go to Italy, but no doubt your Husband would not give his Permission for so Bold a Venture,*" she wrote. I was filled with a wild excitement. To get away from Pless, even Andrew whose sight caused me nothing but grief, for a while! To see Italy, the land of music and of art! I could not wait to ask my husband when he should come home. I took the letter and hurried down to him at the plantings, to see what he would say.

He was working at a place near the centre. He had a phial in his hand with which he was dabbing at the new scars where side-branches had been pruned to allow for straight growth. Saginaw, his back turned to me, was sawing up the sturdy cuttings for firewood. I stared for moments at his muscular golden back, seeing, not for the first time, what had drawn Penuel to him; he still had a kind of animal beauty. Or had I myself changed? Had my feeling for my husband revealed new sensations in me?

I showed Andrew the letter; he frowned a little, I thought at being disturbed. "If it will divert you, go," he told me. The tears rushed to my eyes, which was not reasonable; had he refused me permission, would I not have had the more cause to weep? He set down the phial on the ground, and turned to me.

"Saginaw will soon be off on his travels, for he has worked here half the year," he told me. "I myself have to go to London within the next few weeks, to see my lords of the Admiralty. Whether they will come here or not remains to be seen. But in the meantime the children are left alone with servants. That I mislike, but their company has never meant anything to you; nor has mine."

What devil entered me? I should have told him that his company, and his heart, if he would give it me, meant everything on earth. But I turned on my heel, and said "I may go, then?"

"You may go. I wish you a pleasant journey, Primrose. If my lords of the Admiralty come, they must dine at the inn."

He was smiling. I did not answer, and hurried off, scarce

able to see where I went for tears. What follies the human heart can conjure! Had he asked me to go with him to London, I would readily enough have jettisoned the Duchess and her travelling-plans. But he had not asked me, and doubtless never would: it was increasingly evident that our lives lay along separate paths. I was almost certain, in my own mind, about the other woman concerning whom I had already had suspicions. Who could blame him? And yet—

I hurried back to my room, and began to look through my wardrobe for the journey. At least such an occupation would take my thoughts from myself, and my wretched and incurable state of being in love with my own husband.

I could fill many books concerning Italy, so I will speak of it briefly. I had never before pictured Florence, with its bell-tower and its bronze cathedral gates and a hundred other wonders including the Bridge of Sighs, where suicides drop into the river; and afterwards Venice and the glorious sunsets over the Adriatic, which I longed to paint but knew I could never do so. We travelled in Venetian gondolas, and saw the paintings of Titian and Tintoretto and the many great water-side palaces marked with damp from the canals. We saw the lions of St. Mark's, and then journeyed north again to Lombardy to find the poplars already yellow with spring. All this time I had not heard from home, and had not written. I bought embroidered jackets for the boys from a Swiss traveller who had carried down such work from his native mountains, as well as wooden carvings to take to Rome and sell. I tried also to be an obliging companion to the Duchess, who—and it surprised me that I had not thought of such a matter before—was as lonely as I. But she did not discuss her solitude, nor I mine.

At nights I would sometimes lie awake in the strange beds and stare at the wall-lamps floating in oil as they had done since Roman times. I would think of Andrew, myself, our life, in the light of the broadened experience this journey had given my ignorance. It came to me increasingly how ill I had rewarded his kindness, and I blushed for myself in the night. Brooding on the past is useless unless one can turn it to profit, and I determined that, if the opportunity were given me, I would be a new and better wife to Andrew, erasing the memory of things which had helped to undermine our marriage; my wild and ignorant behaviour at school, my refusal to profit from any teaching I received there or, to the full extent, from that of Miss Minney and Miss Jule. I recalled the way Mary and I had mocked Andrew that time of the summer-holiday; how cruel we had been! And after that I had refused to behave as a wife should, even though the initial mistake at Maverick was not my fault. I could see enough fault in all the rest hardly to excuse myself even that. Had I perhaps made eyelash-play at Harry Clun? Had I encouraged him?

All my bad deeds came back to torment me time and again, leaving me wretched. I often thought of writing to Andrew and twice I started a letter, but it was sadly inadequate and did not begin to convey what I felt, and on both occasions I tore the letters to fragments and watched them float away on the water beyond the window. By day I banished such thoughts in an effort to try to be good company for the Duchess. "You are a young rattle," she told me once, so I may have succeeded. She was a woman who had learned long ago to be sufficient to herself; she did not ask for the pomp she could have had in abundance, but preferred, as in the old days at Maverick when she had snipped roses in an old straw hat, to walk about quietly looking at paintings, or alterpieces, or famous buildings. She knew much about all of these, and gave me the benefit of her instruction, so by the end I was at least less of an ignoramus than at the beginning. I began to see that the genteel education the Lawnmarket had tried to provide was a shallow thing, and that this, that I was now experiencing, was the deeper and truer by far. But no doubt I was fortunate in being abroad, and with such a companion.

Occasionally the Duchess would meet an acquaintance from England, for in those days many like her grew restless and went to foreign countries, before war came. I would listen to their informed, gallant talk and then look at the big solitary woman and think of the wreck of her marriage and how she had not even been able to bear children to give it purpose. Then I would reflect that I had allowed my own children little purpose in my life, and they did not love me; and so tormented myself again, like a squirrel on a wheel. I began, in fact, to long to be home, no matter what fresh griefs awaited me there. I would look at the blue hard foreign sky and long for the rain about Pless. Perhaps this is the way the exiles felt, who had fought for their king and lost their lands: at least I still had mine to which to return, but I did not know how long our present journey would last and it seemed discourteous in me to be the one to suggest an ending to it.

But chance favoured me. One day the Duchess said "Primrose, I have a fancy to travel south again, and return to Rome. There is an English colony there."

"My grandfather was one of them; alas, he is now dead."

She had not known my grandfather, but continued in her even voice with its hint of hidden laughter. "It no longer matters whether or not one visits the Pretender, so I shall do so. There was a time when the British Ambassador, Sir Horace Mann, sent home reports of everyone who paid him respect, so that when they returned they were not received at Court with any favour. But all that is over and done with, as he can have no heirs. Will you come, or do you feel that you must return to your husband and children? I have no wish to keep you from them, pleasant though your company is to me."

I thought for moments how it would also have been pleasant to meet those who had perhaps known my grandfather and my mother, but from the beginning I knew what my answer would be. I said "Ma'am, you have been very good to me and I have seen places and sights I shall never forget. But I—"

She smiled, and broke in. "You think it is time to be going home, eh? Well, you are young; your Andrew is a fortunate man. I was sorry that there was no leisure to make his acquaintance that time at Maverick. I have always admired him for laying my nephew Harry Clun flat."

I gasped at the onyx stare, which held amusement in its depths. Very little missed the Duchess of Croy.

We made our separate arrangements for departure and the Duchess found—there were always such persons for Her Grace to find—a young English governess who was returning home, and who would act as companion to me on the journey. We parted affectionately, the Duchess leaving in a bustle of hampers and other luggage for Rome, whereas I travelled north with my subdued compatriot. I thanked God that He had never seen fit to put me in such a situation as having to teach other people's children. It seems to impose a constant state of servitude, loss of all humour, and fear of being noticed or seduced.

I reached Pless three weeks later, and at once asked if my husband were at home. Then I saw my own letter, written from Southampton, lying unopened on a tray, and my heart sank. Bethia gaped at me. "The master is from home, ma'am," she said, "gone to Lunnon he is five days since, not knowing you would return, for there is the letter." She knew my handwriting. The bitter thought that Andrew and I had been in London at the same time, passing in opposite directions, was not lost on me. However, there was no help for it and I must await his return. I suddenly felt very tired; it had been a long journey. I gave Bethia my hat and cloak and directed her about the baggage, and asked for food to be sent me, though I did not feel like eating, in my room.

Two days later a visitor came. I could hardly believe my ears when Bethia announced Lord Harry Clun. His effrontery in coming to my very door was proof that Andrew was known to be from home, I thought. I told Bethia to say that I was not receiving. Shortly she returned.

"Ma'am, the gentleman—his lordship—says he has news of great import which must be told only to yourself. He entreats that you will see him."

I moved nearer the bell-cord. "Very well, show him in," I said coldly, and was standing in my place when Clun entered, dressed in riding-clothes. He came forward to kiss my hand, but I would not extend it. There was even more confidence about him than was customary, and I liked him even less. If only Andrew were here!

"I had no wish to see you," I said. "If I were not known to be alone here, you would never have come."

"Goddess—"

"Do not call me by that ridiculous name. State your business, then be gone."

"Primrose, then; you leave me no choice. I only learned of your return yesterday evening, when it was too late to call."

He smiled, and began to walk up and down, with his eyes always on me. "I would have waited even longer to impart such news as I have," he said. "As I told you, it is for your private ear alone. Dismiss your servant, I beg, from outside the door, where she undoubtedly lingers."

I did not reply and turned and walked instead into the window-embrasure. "You may speak with confidence here," I said in a low voice. What his news might be I did not greatly care, but was anxious to be rid of him; his pale eyes shone with the wild light I recalled from Maverick, and he seemed elated beyond his everyday impudence.

He came to a standstill, the smile still playing about his lips. "I wonder if you will presently admit to yourself how much I have you in my power?" he said. "Believe me, I shall make it clear to you."

"I am waiting for the fact of your presence to be made clear, for it was my wish that you should be kept out." He laughed softly; nothing I said appeared to make an impression on him. I frowned a little; what could be this matter of such import? "Have done with mystery," I said. "I am not alone here, as I was at Maverick; my servants are within call."

"Servants will not avail you." He was savouring his moment, standing on the balls of his feet and then subsiding again, like an insect stretching its legs. I loathed him in that moment as I had never done before. "Will they not?" I said. "What is this great matter?" If he did not come to it soon, I thought, I would withdraw. He said then "Thornton, you see, is— careless."

"What has that to do with me, if so?" It was true enough about Thornton, I knew. Clun laughed outright. "He does not turn his attention sufficiently to what might profit him, or spend enough time searching his mother's papers."

"That is a matter for Thornton to repair; why come to me?" I was beginning, however, to be alarmed. It seemed as if the creature were about to blackmail me, though I could not think of any grounds he might have. Again I wished that Andrew were near.

"May we sit?" suggested Clun affably. I said that I should prefer to remain standing, and he replied "As you will. To be brief, then I won a jewel-case from Thornton some time ago at play. It had belonged to his mother, and as I suspected contained little jewellery. What there was of value, Thornton would long ago have sold." He sat down, and again stretched his legs, in their knee-high boots, so that the attitude was an insult. "He had pledged himself beyond the hilt to me already, and is my host," he continued. "I accepted the offer of the box for whatever it might contain. I was not ill-rewarded."

"Give any jewels there may be to your poor wife," I said. "She must have small joy of you."

He flushed in an ugly fashion. "You will regret your sharp tongue."

"I doubt it," I said flippantly, adding that aunt Milhall had always worn jet.

"I have already hinted that the matter is not one of jewellery. There were none of any value; but I examined the box thoroughly, as is my way. Women, especially old ones, have secret places where they keep matters they consider of importance, at least to themselves. In this case, the matter went further. It was a letter; no, no, not a love letter; nothing so frivolous; I know your mind."

I was cold. "If you found a document, you should return it to Thornton, not myself, if that was your intention."

"Were I to return it to Thornton, my dear, you and your husband and children would be without a roof to cover you, and all Farquharson's famous trees would belong to your kinsman."

I felt the blood leave my face. "What is it you mean to tell me? I do not understand."

"You will soon do so. I am not unreasonable towards your husband; the man has worked hard, and should reap the reward of his many years' labour. I bear him no grudge for having taken me unawares. But now I return blow for blow."

I cannot describe the gloating quality of his last phrase. I would not heed it, I thought. "What did you find?" I said carelessly, my fingers beginning to pull at the curtain-loops on the shutter. The pattern of their stuff showed leaves and cornflowers. I should never forget its last detail. Calm your beating, I told my heart; it may well be the man is lying; he finds it easy. Yet, within myself, I knew he was not. Whatever was to come now would be the truth.

He spoke. "I found a certificate of marriage between your father, James Tebb, and a woman whose name was Beatrice Elmay. The date of the certificate was five years prior to that of your own birth, which I know because I have troubled to find it out. In plain words, my pretty, you are a bastard, and have no heirship of Pless, nor has your husband any rights over it at all."

The blood had returned to my face, to my heart: I left pulling at the loops, and turned and faced him. "This may be a black lie, an invention," I told him. "Who else knows of it? Where is the paper now?"

"To my knowledge, none knows, except Beatrice Tebb herself. I found her, you see. She was once a maidservant at Pless, and held her honour high. Your father paid her an allowance provided she did not reveal the marriage, but at his death the allowance ceased. She was pleased enough to talk, in exchange for silver. If it is needed she will give evidence under oath, before a magistrate. She must have been a comely woman once. She lives modestly enough, in a small cottage where she can eke out a living with washing and goffer-irons. You ask who else knows? No one, and none shall, except yourself and me, if you are reasonable."

"What do you want?" I knew that, so near the time of sale of the trees, Andrew must not learn of this. He would be honest enough to inform Thornton and no doubt lose all that he had worked for these many years. And I would have done this to him, I who had never, since he married me, been other than a dragging expense and cause of mischief! Now, there was only one way to save him. But I must be sure; I must have that paper, and be certain there was no copy.

"Yourself, Primrose. Have I ever pretended otherwise? You cannot call me devious."

"I call you a knave and villain. How am I to know that even given myself, you would not trick me? Have you the paper with you? Would you give it me if I . . ."

"I will give you nothing until I have what I desire. Then— I do not strike a hard bargain, Primrose, I will give it into your keeping the first night I am in your bed—then you shall have it, and I will have your body, which pleases us both."

"Please me?" I said. "I would as soon bed with a toad," and I did not add that even this was too great a compliment, for I have always liked toads, with their jewelled eyes. Besides, they do harm to none, and this man was evil. An adder would have been a likelier comparison. But his eyes had hardened and it was plain he did not like my manner of speech.

"I will teach you courtesy, my sweet, when. . . . But when is it to be? Tonight? I have waited very long, and would not further prolong the waiting."

"How am I to know that you will not . . . will not . . ." My mind was growing confused with horror. Were I to become his mistress for one night only, I thought, were he to give me the paper, there were still church registers. The marriage would be entered there. Clun would have been certain to find out where the entry was, in order to torment me. One night would not be enough for him; I must be his mistress till he tired of me, and then trust to his lack of interest in not making the thing plain to all. Besides, by then the trees would have been sold. I should have saved Andrew's interest in Pless. After that, it did not matter.

"Tonight?" said Harry Clun again. He was staring at the cleft between my breasts and his hand stroked my arm. I dared not withdraw. As he had said, I was in his power. After he had left, I felt, I would go to my room and vomit. And tonight? But I must not think of that before I need.

# Twenty-eight

THERE WAS A DOOR which led from the grounds, by way of a straight flight of steps, to the tower wing where I slept. I had oiled the lock and taken out the key.

The dark had fallen. I had lit three candles in a sconce as we had arranged, and placed them near the window. I did this without thought, for I had no mind for anything now. Where my brain had been was frozen. I hardly spared a thought for my wretched father and the way in which my mother and grandfather had been befooled, in a worse manner even than they knew. That last was a blessing. Nor could I think of Andrew—him least of all—and as regarded what was to come, I did not contemplate it.

I had undressed and wrapped a bed-gown round myself, telling myself it was what whores would wear, easy to strip off.

Earlier in the day I had gone to Andrew's study where he kept his accounts. I could not have borne to look at these, or to picture his neat careful hand filling in the columns, each item noted. Instead I had gone to the place where he kept his pistols and had taken them out and balanced the deadly, perfect things in my hands, and had laid one against my cheek and put the other back in its case. I dared not take the pistol upstairs with me. I would not kill myself—that would accomplish nothing, and I still had the will for survival—but I might well kill Clun. So I put both pistols back where I had found them, and went out of the room, closing the door carefully. I prayed that Andrew might sit there at his work-table again and never know what I had done to make it possible for him to continue. If I could no longer respect myself, it must be possible for him to respect me. His love I would no longer merit. Again the clouds in my mind descended, making known things hard to remember. If only I could forget this night!

I heard footsteps on the staircase, and rose to my feet. Presently the door opened and Clun came in. I felt the loathing rise in my throat, and downed it. Whatever befell, I must endure him now.

I had taken up the candles and they were between us. "Give me the paper," I said to him. He smiled, eyeing me in the way I hated as I hated every part of him, body and soul. "What, Primrose? Must I pay you before I have made you sing for your supper? And that you shall do, by God."

He made to come at me and I took a firmer grip on the sconce. "You shall have your due," I told him. "But first I must read the paper and burn it to ashes. At least I will know then that. . . ." Words failed me. He came to me and pressed a kiss carelessly on my arm above the elbow, then felt in his bosom and brought out a folded paper which he tucked into my palm. "As you will," he said. "I have played fairly by you, Primrose; do you the same by me."

"You shall have your due," I said again. I laid down the sconce and unfolded the paper and read it by candlelight. It was a true certificate of marriage; he had not lied. Below my father's name and the woman's I noted the parish; Thursby in Yorkshire. Then I held the paper to the candle-flame and watched it curl, then blaze. When at last it burnt my fingers I dropped it to the floor and ground it to dust with my foot.

"And now," said Lord Harry Clun.

He strode over, seizing the bed-gown and ripping it off me. I stood naked, and at the sight he laid hold of me and, pulling me into his arms, began to tear and bite with his teeth at my flesh, my breasts and shoulders. Between kissing and tearing he carried me to the bed. He did not speak again but began to undo the fastenings of his own clothes, his breeches-buttons, the tying of his shirt. When he was naked he came to me. He was long and pale and thin like a plant that has not had enough of the sun; I could smell his acrid sweat.

I was deadly cold, in mind and body. I could watch the thing that was to be done to me as though it happened to someone else. I felt him mount, lie astride me on the bed; I felt its mattress give beneath our double weight, man and woman. I remember thinking "Here I am lying naked with Harry Clun," and felt his member extend itself and harden to take me, and my own withdrawal. I myself, Primrose Farquharson, was somewhere watching all of this, as once long ago I had watched my fate settled from Pless gallery; as once, again, I had watched Penuel and the Indian lying together in a wood. The clear thought came then "When Andrew returns, if this affair is not over, the house will not be safe for Clun and myself. We will have to meet in the woods or on a concealed place in the marsh, and lie there."

I felt Clun's flesh against me; it was as hot as my own was cold. He was still kissing and fondling, thrusting his tongue between my lips, my teeth. He had entered me. Presently he would begin to ride and thrust.

Then I looked up and saw Andrew in his riding-clothes standing in the doorway, white about the mouth. I gave a great cry and kicked out and made Clun roll off me, roll by himself on to the floor.

## Twenty-nine

I HAD COME BACK to myself, to my own body: I clutched the
covers round me to hide my naked flesh. Beyond the bed, Clun
was trying to rise. Andrew let him scramble to his knees and
then launched out another such blow as I remembered, sending
him crashing to the floor. He did this again and again, till
Clun began to cry and swear, with blood running from his nose
and mouth. The obscenities ran on for seconds, then Andrew,
his lips tight, came to where Clun's clothes lay and threw
them to him where he lay crouched on the floor.

"This is not done with," Andrew said.

I heard the sound of sobbing; it was my own. Neither man
looked towards me or made as if he heard me. I watched them
go out together, Clun meanwhile stumbling into his breeches
and shirt. The door shut. I got myself off the bed and found
my slippers, and crept into the bedgown I had been wearing
when Clun came in. There might be murder done, I knew, and
I must stop it; somehow, anyhow. It depended on whether they
used their fists or their swords or pistols.

The pistols! I remembered leaving them downstairs in the
study. I hurried out of the room and down by way of the

corridor which led to the main part of the house. The men had gone, out by the lower doorway. I reached the study door at last and found the place and, thank God, the case of pistols was still where I had left it, and I took it with me back to my room. I hid the case in the clothes-chest and then went down the tower stairs, almost running, hearing my own sobbing breath. The moon had not risen but there was bright starlight, and I could see my way.

I could hear nothing at all. I stopped for moments, my hand to my breast. Wherever they had gone, whatever form the punishment was taking, it was nowhere within sight or hearing. Presently I heard the sound of hoofbeats, slow and growing fainter in the distance. My heart thudded: it was over, evidently. Was Andrew hurt, lying somewhere in the plantings?

I started to go to find him, but did not have to travel far. He came to me, his face drawn and cold in the starlight. He said to me "Get back to your room." He might have been speaking to a stranger. I stayed where I was and said "For God's sake tell me; did you use swords?" For they might have done so, in the heat of the moment, without seconds. At least my husband was not wounded, if so.

"I would not soil a sword for such a cause." His tone was like ice. He was breathing fast, as though he had been running. I tried to keep my mind from panic; I knew they could not have used Andrew's pistols; as for the other's, if he had brought them, there had been no shot. My action in hiding Andrew's pair seemed suddenly childish. I would put them back in the morning. "What did you do?" I asked, trying to keep my voice level; it had risen high, like a child's.

"Do? I horsewhipped him. He will not come here again."

It was casually stated, as if he had beaten a dog. My hands flew to my mouth. "He will revenge himself," I said, thinking of Clun's title and his honour, such as it was, and the time-hallowed custom of avenging an insult. "He—he will challenge you, when he is recovered, and send seconds, and—"

"Not he. I doubt if he will ever speak of this night's work, sent home flung across the saddle as he was, like a load of wood. But *you*—"

He jerked his head suddenly, as though giving orders to the dog he had beaten. I followed the way his glance had led; I was to slink back to my room, to receive my own punishment. I went obediently.

I began to be frightened, climbing the stairs. I could hear his tread behind me, and knew that whatever was to happen would be done without loss of time. Then it would be over, at least. My fear was not the fear I had known on coming out into the silent starlight. *That* was over. Nor did I try to say a single word to save myself, to beg or plead. What could there be to say? I could not tell him of the burnt paper. I could tell him nothing, nothing at all, till after the trees were sold.

I reached my room and he followed me inside and closed the door, leaning against it and looking at me.

"So you are a whore," he said. "I had not thought that of you, I must confess; your faults lay otherwise, as far as I knew. But I found Clun's mount in the stable."

"I am not—" But his look silenced me. I would not speak again. Nor could I weep, nor would it help me. There was no help, and he must do as he would. At least I was rid of Clun.

He spoke again, turning away. "I'll not tame your flesh with the whip I used for your paramour tonight, for it is used to spur honest mares." He had taken off his coat, hanging it carefully on the peg behind the door. He looked at me. "Take that gown off," he said, "there is no need to have it torn in ribbons."

He watched while I laid aside the gown. As I did so I had a hope—hardly that, only a gleam of a likelihood, one chance against many—that the sight of my nakedness would partly assuage his anger. I was again very pretty, with my flower-petal flesh and breasts still small and high despite the fact that

I had borne his children. But another part of my mind knew it was useless to hope for mercy. My knees began to tremble as I stood there, while Andrew took off his belt. It was made of heavy black leather, used for holding knives and sometimes guns while he worked in the woods. He always wore it.

"Turn round," he said, "and lean over the bed."

"Andrew, I—"

There was no answer, save the heavy swish of the belt through the air. I had flung my arm up to protect my face and the blow hit it, knocking the arm senseless as I fell across the bed the way he bade me. The next blow caught me squarely across the buttocks and I bit my lip hard. I felt the belt come down again and again; each time it strapped me across the flesh, with a spare blow now and again for the back, another for the sides, and the after-flick catching at my arms above the elbow. I had crammed both fists against my mouth and presently bunched a part of the coverlet and stuffed it in, so that if I cried out he would not hear me. All the time I was thinking "Primrose, this is for what you did long ago; if you did not deserve to be beaten for tonight, there's the time you mocked him—the times you would not lie with him and made him force you—the time you went out walking against his orders and hurried the birth—the time you made herbs,"— oh, oh, I can think no more, he is hurting, he is hurting me. . . .

He stopped, got his coat and blundered out. Before the door shut he said over his shoulder "That is the medicine for little whores." Then he was gone and I was alone with my bruised body. I was aware of an overwhelming desire, despite the pain, that he should have stayed and made love to me. But he had not: had not wanted to.

I tried to put on the bedgown again but it hurt my flesh. I doused the candles—could they have been burning all this time?—and dragged myself to the window, staring at the night beyond. Across the garden was a blackness which rose almost to the stars; the trees. I had saved the trees for Andrew.

*I doubt if he will ever speak of this night's work.* And the paper was burnt. If only it could be true that Clun would accept his defeat, and do no more harm! If only he did not tell Thornton that he was the real owner of the land, now it was worth having! Aunt Milhall must have suppressed that truth as long as Pless was a liability. She had let Andrew marry me knowing the inheritance was a lie. She had thought of Pless as a derelict place that would drag on the market, which would be of no use to her son, would involve him in debt like my father's had been.

The land. Pless. And I had been the bargain, the surety. I was still so. It was not possible to forget that tonight Andrew had hurt me. Yet with every part of my flesh crying out, I was proud of him. Andrew did nothing badly; he had made Pless pay, he had made Clun pay . . . and myself. I laid my cheek on my arms against the sill while childhood phrases drifted through my mind. A sound thrashing. A good whipping. You'll eat your breakfast standing (this had been one of aunt Milhall's phrases, after some nursery punishment). Tomorrow. . . .

I crawled into my bed at last and gingerly pulled the covers over me, lying on my stomach. Now I could cry, in little short bursts; not for the beating. Would I ever be able to explain to Andrew how it had all of it happened? But not now, not yet. The bruised blood beat in me to the sound of that: not yet, till the trees are sold.

Next morning I was determined to face him, seat myself as usual, as though nothing had happened, and pour out his coffee for breakfast and ask about his journey. There was nothing else to be done if we were to continue to live in the same house together. It would be incredible, as things were, if the servants had guessed nothing, with Harry Clun's horse impudently stabled and, later, limping away with its burden into the night. I must give the lie to gossip; try to make

Andrew proud of me. Proud? Perhaps not yet; but later, when he knew. . . .

Somehow I writhed into my clothes and caught my breath with pain as I laced my stays, adjusted my garters. My arms felt stiff as I lifted them to comb my hair and I was astonished to see my face in the mirror unmarked, and as usual, except for a heaviness about the eyes. So much to the good; as for sitting down, it was not easy.

There was a knock at the door and Bethia entered, with a tray. She said "The master says as you're to have your breakfast sent up, ma'am, seeing you was poorly in the night." I made my lips smile acceptance while my mind howled its disappointment. Poorly in the night! And he did not want to see me. I would make a pretence of eating, I thought; and drank some coffee.

A note was lying on the tray. My heart thumped, and I waited until Bethia had crossed the room before opening it; if there were an answer, she could take it. One thing it was certain not to be, and that was an apology. Like most women, odd creatures that we are, this would have disappointed me. But it was no such thing. It was cold and formal, lacking a heading, with only the date.

*"My Lords of the Admiralty are to dine here on Tuesday, which is the Reason for my Hurried Arrival Home. I took it for Granted, as you Formerly Spoke of it, that you would Contrive some sort of a Supper, as Several will come. They will be out with me all of the Day, and will be staying some at the Inn, some with the Admiral, as they would not come here for the Trouble. However I promised them Dinner, so I ask Again that you will Make a Showing."*

No more; only his initials, A.F. Well, I would get their meal for them if it killed me, which after all his beating had not. I turned to Bethia. "Tell your master that will be in order," I said, and as soon as she had departed made haste to get up off my screaming backside. It was still raw, and would be scarce cooled, I did not doubt, by Tuesday.

# Thirty

MY LORDS of the Admiralty Gosse and Ingestre, with a suitably frogged and braided attendance, came to dine after seeing the trees in Andrew's forest, to which they must give their final seal of approval before the purchase was made fact. All day they had tramped about, supported by their sticks (Lord Gosse had gout) and their lieutenants. Andrew went with them, which gave me leisure to put the final touches to the dinner-table and to make the pastry-balls for the Carlton House soup, which I had ventured to try. I was pleased with the meal which they would eat and hoped they would do it justice: a raised hare pie, roast mutton, sucking pig with butter-sauce and sage, veal collops, eels in cream, and a great Gloucester cheese to finish before the port, which I had left to Andrew to provide. I trusted that he would be pleased with what I had done, for we had hardly spoken three words together since the terrible night of Clun's visit, and even those not in private. But perhaps, if all went well over the trees and it was helped down by a good dinner, he would forgive me at least in part. I busied myself, at any rate, and hardly left time to dress myself and powder my hair, for tonight was to be a grand occasion.

When I came downstairs to greet my lords I could see that they found me a pleasant sight and were prepared to be agreeable, even gallant. This pleased me, for with some trouble I had hidden the bruises on my arms with lace, and managed my fan and skirts so as to hide them, and moreover, the fact that even by now I could barely sit down without wincing. At the table they did the food full justice, and old Lord Ingestre, who had a purple face like a damson, said to me "Why, ma'am, ye have better cooks in this part of the world than London, to be sure; I'd be fain to tempt yours south for a fee, save that it would inconvenience so fair a lady, to lose her. A fortunate man, our host; a lovely wife, a first-rate cook, and, damn me, a forest the like of which has never before been seen in all England. I congratulate ye, Farquharson."

I smiled and waved my fan back and forth, not claiming credit for the meal, for I knew that in fashionable circles no lady was aware of what went on in her kitchen. But I hoped Andrew did not lay all the credit on Bethia. That would be unlucky for me; but I was pleased to hear the old gentleman say perhaps more than he ought to have said about the trees, before the Admiralty deliberations when he finally returned south. These elderly lords had seen most of the world's marvels, I thought, if indeed they had ever been to sea; and they still seemed to think Andrew's trees worth mention. I was happy for *him*; he sat still and quiet in the candlelight, at last, toying with the walnuts on his plate, and I rose, curtsied, and left them, with the admirals turning after me with glasses raised. Yes, Andrew might forgive me much for this night, I thought. I did not wait for the men to come up, for I was very weary and I knew they would spend many hours over their port, talking of tenders and contracts.

Next day Andrew thanked me for my trouble, formally and unsmiling. "They have promised the contract?" I exclaimed. He smiled a little, and I thought his eyes looked tired.

"A promise is worth nothing save in writing, but I have hopes that that will be sent in due course. Meantime, the trees are to be cut. They will grow no more, and when—if—the order comes to send them south, they must be ready."

I clasped my hands together to still their shaking. "What will you find to employ your leisure?" I said to him. "You have spent eight years on those trees, scarcely stopping to sleep or eat."

"Eight years from the seed, it is true. I also have some business in Canada which merits more of my attention than it has had: of that I would speak to you when we have more time, and are alone."

His voice was still cold. I turned away and busied myself with putting away the dishes from last night's meal, for some stayed always in the sideboard in the great hall, being too seldom used for the kitchen. As always, I noticed how little we had in the way of silver, china or even pewter since my father's day. All had gone then to pay the creditors, and what we had had been bought in cheaply, over the years, by Andrew at the booths in Edinburgh and elsewhere. A curious thought struck me at that moment; I was glad I had used Miss Jule's great pan for some of the cooking yesterday. She would have approved the feast and been glad for Andrew's sake that matters had seemed to go favourably for him.

I firmed my lips, which like my hands were beginning to tremble. Would he never forgive me? I dreaded to hear what he would have to say about Canada; if he went abroad now, I thought, it would break my heart.

It was worse than that; much worse.

We met in the small drawing-room, where I sometimes sat sketching. He came in quietly and closed the door and said "Put down what you are at, Primrose. I have a matter to discuss, which will not take many moments; but I have been wondering about the wisdom of it as events have turned out."

The blue eyes were hard. "Had you not been as you are I would have said it had been safe, as we have no joy in one another's company, to take the boys with me and live on in Canada, leaving you to your own devices. But when these include whoring, with Clun or another, how can I go abroad with a clear mind? I'd not have my name dragged in the mud, nor those of our sons, while I am out of the country."

I had given a great cry: and suddenly knew I could bear no more. I recall saying it aloud, with my hands over my face.

"I cannot bear it, I cannot bear it!"

Still he did not move. "What cannot you bear?" he said reasonably. "I do not flatter myself that it is my departure you dread; and you have never shown affection for the children."

"You do not understand—you do not know—"

"Then tell me what it is I do not understand," he said sternly. "I think I do so only too well. As soon as I am elsewhere, you invite your lover to this house; you, who I had thought were at least chaste even as a part of your fault, for you have never been a loving wife to me. As I told you years ago, I am no monk; that I have lived as one is because I have had no time for anything but work, and that hard enough, and seldom ceasing. But you, my wife, are after all no nun, and although I had thought you lived so—"

"I did live so. I have never been unfaithful to you in thought or act." I had turned away, knowing I would hear him laugh; when the sound came, it was hard and mirthless. I was suddenly aware that Andrew had aged since the night he had found me with Clun; he was older, harsher. If I looked at him I would see, I knew, streaks of grey in his bright hair, new lines about his eyes and mouth that the sunlight had not put there. But I dared not look, to betray myself. How he would mock if I were to tell him I loved him!

"We are wasting time," he said drily. "Of the matter of Canada—"

I flung about, letting him see my tear-stained face. "You

have all the time in the world now, have you not? There is nothing to do but cut the trees—and burn the undergrowth—and then be off, leaving a ruined place behind you; Pless has served you well enough and now you are rid of it, and myself."

"Maybe you have served me less well than the land." But his tone was softening; it could not be possible for Andrew to prolong unkindness, unless he had changed more greatly than I knew.

He came over suddenly, setting his hands on my arms. I winced slightly, and he raised the lace fall at my elbow; below it there was a bruise. "I hurt you, it is true," he said. "I am sorry."

"You thought I deserved it—you thought—"

"Your demeanour is not that of a guilty woman," he said, puzzled, "but with Clun in your very chamber, on your bed—"

"There was a reason for that, which I must not tell you." My own words sounded childish, but he did not smile.

"Then if you must not tell it me, it cannot be one I need credit." He led me to a chair. "Come, sit down; you have had a weary week, and I know—yes, I know how hard you worked preparing our dinner. It may have sold the trees; one never knows how such things will affect the lords of creation."

"If they are certainly sold—" My mind was clearing; I gripped the chair-arms with my fists. Could I go on longer? Could I, could any woman, be expected to lose husband, love, children, good name, all for the price of dead wood?

"'Certainly' is a word I'd not use with their lordships; they take a long time to come to decisions, but it will do them no good for the trees to lie rotting, and if they have a grain of sense they will write soon. Primrose, I know there is something you would say to me. Say it, I beg, without fear of my anger. I have maybe used you hardly of late—and too softly before. It may be that the fault is mine. But you were twelve years old when I married you, and unfit to be a wife."

"You think I am unfit still," I said, and burst into noisy sobbing.

He came to me. "Have I said so? It is only your way with the children and myself, and that night with Clun—"

"Do you suppose I could not have lain down in the lanes with Clun any day while our mounts cropped grass together? He was at me for a year and more before he—before he forced me to it. I may tell you that, I believe, though you don't credit what I say. And he scarce had time to lie with me."

"I do not say you are untruthful. It was against what I thought of as your whole nature; that is what made me angry. How could he force you to let him in? You were safe in this house, were you not? Yet you had to turn the key, and open to him."

"It was—by reason of something he knew, and had evidence of."

"Some misdemeanour of your own?" He frowned. I scrubbed at my tears with my fists, as I had done when a child.

"Must you always blame me? There was no misdemeanour either of yours or mine."

"Then what—"

"What he knew would have destroyed your life, the land, the trees, everything you value. Is that not enough?"

"Then he still knows it," he said quietly. I gripped my hands together. "Have no fear," I said, "I've destroyed the evidence."

"What evidence?"

"A piece of paper. To buy it I had to sell my honour, or would have had to had you not come in. You were in too much haste, I daresay, to note the charred dust lying on the floor. By now, alas, it is swept away."

"So the devil blackmailed you, and you—" He had moved nearer to me. He put out his hand, as if to take mine in it. But I was still crying, and would not accommodate him.

"I insist on knowing all of it," he said. I felt his fingers under my chin trying to raise my face. He raised it, blotched and unseemly as it was; and smiled. He always smiled when I least expected it. I sniffed and thought to myself how lately it had seemed that he would never smile at me again.

"Tell me," said Andrew, "and we will share our tears if we must. I can see that you have suffered when I knew nothing of it. I should have given you more time to speak the other night; I was wrong to treat you as I did, in haste and anger."

"What you saw was enough excuse," I gulped; the sobs were still rising. "I had meant not to tell you any more. It is wrong of me, because I know you—I know you will—"

"Will what?" he said. I stared at him fiercely. He was smiling still, his eyes intent on my face, which God knows cannot have been a pleasant sight all streaked with tears. "I cannot be hurt more greatly than when I thought you a whore," he said. "Forgive me, Primrose. Whatever you have to say now, I know now that you were never that. Will this console you?"

"I would have been a whore, for your sake. I know what you love best in the world, and I cannot—I cannot bear that you should lose it through me." That was as far as I need go, I thought; the rest he need not know, or suspect, till the trees were sold. But his next words threw me off balance very much.

"What I love best in the world," he said, "is a stubborn little creature with a head all over curls, a cool hand for pastry and a hot intemperate choler for all things else. Now—"

"You love me?" I said. "Did you say you loved me?"

He came and picked me up and set me on his knee. I turned my face into his coat and wept and wept. Then I began kissing him all over his face. I daresay he liked it, because he kissed me back.

How could I have held out against him in the end? Of course I did not; now I knew he loved me—I should have seen it earlier—matters were quite different. Besides, it was still possible that the news would reach him through Thornton and Clun. So I told him of Clun's letter and how he had threatened to show it to Thornton, and how aunt Milhall must have kept it in case it should be needed, and meantime made use of Andrew to pay off Pless's debt. "But if there should be a lawsuit, Thornton will win," I sobbed, "and after all your work—and marrying me for the land which was never mine—"

"It was the worst day's work I ever put in." He was caressing the back of my neck with one hand, while the other arm held me close. A great burden of fear was lifted from me and I felt as light as air. I was no longer afraid; Andrew knew of everything; the weight of it was lifted from my shoulders and did not seem as if it were unduly troubling his. But there was another thing. I laid my cheek against his and began to tell him of Penuel and Saginaw, because I could not bear that in this moment there should be any estrangement between us, and I remembered that he had told me I was like a nun, and I was no nun, any more than he was a monk. So I told him of Penuel and the Indian and how he had smeared ashes on her foot and then locked the door, and how I had seen them later in the wood and seen her come home in the dawn and had afterwards gone with her to the abortionist, and in the end watched her die of it. "I told no one," I said. "I have never told anyone but you. But I cannot bear that you think I do not love you," and I rubbed my smooth cheek against his rough one, for no matter how carefully a man shaves the bristles are always felt. I thought how true it was that I loved Andrew more than anything in the world, and I did not mind that he had loved Penuel first now that there was truth between us.

"Poor Penuel," was all he said, and he gave a sigh. "It is hard to think that she was a mortal woman; only that. As for you—" and he began such kissing of me that I cannot recount it, and it made me very happy and I laughed and cried at the same time, which I have heard of people doing but never thought it possible, till then.

Presently he said "That brings to mind a matter which puzzled me. When I picked up Alexander that day from the bed of bracken—how angry I was with you, my dear love!—I caught sight of something bright between the bed and the wall. I thought it was yours, and brought it with me, but have never had the opportunity to speak of it. It was a garter, of blue silk, somewhat faded."

He turned my face to him again. "And you would have given yourself to Clun, to try to save me?"

"To save the land for you. I know you have other occupations."

"I shall presently have an occupation which outpaces all the rest. And I beat you for it . . . what sort of fellow am I?"

"An honest man. I have never thought you other."

"Then, if I am honest, as you deduced, the trees belong to Thornton."

"Andrew—"

"Never fear, I shall not make him an outright offer. When they are sold, cut and gone, I shall ride over and have a talk with him, and lawyer Arnison with me. I think there may be some little to be saved for ourselves out of this coil, and meantime—"

When he kissed me again I found myself thinking of the blue silk garter. It must have lain between successive layers of bracken ever since Saginaw drew it off Penuel's knee. Then I stopped thinking of garters. I was still amazed, bloated with crying and happy beyond belief. Andrew loved me; nothing else was of importance. If the lawsuit failed I would sail with him to Canada and cook and bake bread and scour skins and fashion rag rugs like the colonial women, and turn all our worn-out clothing into patchwork quilts. And there would be more children. I was not afraid of bearing Andrew's children now. I was not afraid of anything.

We went to bed. I had never in my life had a lady's maid except at Maverick. Now my husband undressed me for himself. His hands were very gentle and I remembered how they could search for and heal scars and diseases in his trees. He kissed my bruises, and said "And I did this," and hid his face for a while against my breasts while I cradled his head in my arms. "I deserved it for other things," I said, and laid my cheek against him. I felt very close to him and he smelled of himself and of pine resin and of sunshine. Outside it was broad day.

"I will kiss every bruise that it may grow better," he said presently, and began. I replied that most of them were improperly situated.

"We will solace them; I will show you how. You are not afraid, darling?" I knew he had understood, despite my halting words, why the story of Penuel had chilled and alienated me from all bodily love. Now I was to be cured. I said "You know I am not afraid."

He laid me on the bed and turned away to undress. Then he came to me. I will not try to describe our loving. It seemed to fold away the years of mistrust and anger, the barren years of waiting for fulfilment that did not come even with the birth of children. Now, I learned all a woman can know of physical love. I had never before experienced the rush of delight that comes to a willing woman when her lover knows what he is at; and many men do not. Andrew knew; not from any wide experience—he had none, other than with myself in our black time years since, when he had been as unhappy as I—but from his nature, which gave always. His youth had been spent in lonely places with the whole of his mind and heart turned to earning a living, and now—

"You should be at your trees," I told him.

"Ma'am, there is only one tree need trouble you at this present."

I laughed. Our loving continued in this mingling of tenderness and laughter. I am indeed sorry for old maids. At the beginning he had said to me "I will hold you gently," and I had hugged him fiercely and answered "No, hurt me. Hold me hard," and clung to him with all my limbs so that we became as nearly one being as two can be; one flesh is often spoken of in marriage-vows, but how many know of it in truth? The truth was now.

Once we were almost interrupted. Distantly, through ecstasy, I heard the clatter of bucket and broom; it was the half-wit girl who helped Bethia and the rest by cleaning the upstairs rooms. I recalled that we were both naked in bed at this hour of the day, and sat up and called out "Phoebe, do not sweep this room today; go back to the kitchen and help them there."

"You know very well how to direct your servants," came the voice from the bed. I flung myself down again and said against him "You are not my servant, as you know well."

"Little wretch. Come here again, come here. . . ."

The clatter had died away. Shortly he said, as if recalling some matter of hours since "There was no fear that she would get in, for I snecked the door." Often the Scots have the only word that will do.

I cannot recall that we ate all that day or did anything except make love. Yet I can remember that we spared time to go and visit the children, and we must have dressed ourselves for that; and Jamie's fingers clutched at the last at my gown, and I got him to smile at me. All that they needed was to know me more, and Andrew sent the nurse away and this made it easier, and we played some game with a toy made of wood and painted yellow. But I can recall nothing clearly except falling asleep in bed again at last in Andrew's arms, happier than I had ever been in all my life. His arms were strong and sheltered me, and I knew that whatever befell they would shelter me always. I could picture us as an old man and an old woman, both strange, precious and yet known to one another. Then I slept, and he did not leave me; I know, for when I awoke it was to find his arms still about me although he was deeply asleep.

Outside the wind had risen: it seemed very far away.

When was it that he had said "I had rather hold you in my arms than grow all the trees in Christendom"? Perhaps it was that night, perhaps later. But I remember the saying, and what it came to mean.

I woke. It was still dark, yet not so, and the wind howled. I stirred against Andrew and was suddenly broad awake, wondering for moments why the darkness was filled with swaying orange light. Then it came to me that there was fire, not in the house, but out there at the plantings. I sat up in bed and saw a great ring of flame soar upwards among the trees. I shook Andrew awake. "The forest is burning," I cried. "Someone has set it on fire." This certainty was with me almost before I had time to think, added to the fact that it had been dry weather.

He was out of bed in a trice and struggling into his breeches. He said to me "Go to the children and see that whatever happens, you and they are safe," and I flung on my bedgown and before he had even gone from the room, had hurried to do his bidding. My mind held no surprise. It was as though this or something like it had been certain to come. We had been too fortunate. Someone, probably Clun, had taken revenge, using to advantage the one day Andrew had not been out at his trees. Not by the sword or pistols, but swiftly in the dry wind-swept dark with a tinder, perhaps with oil, it had been done. I must do what I could now to save Andrew's life-work from the deadly blow it had suffered while he was alone with me. I blamed myself already; so many things had been my fault, and this time I would try to atone.

I hurried first to the nursery, which was in the further part of the house. The boys were asleep; I scarcely took time to glance at them and then went to wake the nurse. She was a sensible Lancashire woman, useful at such a time. "Get their clothes," I told her, "and I will help you to put the pony between the trap-shafts. Drive straight to the Admiral's, tell him what has happened and ask him to send men for aid." The Admiral's was nearer than Mallet, and out of reach of Clun. I left the nurse to carry out her orders, went down to the stables and spoke gently to the already restive pony and got him hitched into the shafts of the trap with sweating, fumbling fingers, while the wind stirred his mane.

"You are coming with us, ma'am?" The nurse was already at my side, with a child, warmly wrapped, at each hand. "No," I said, "take Bethia," for I knew the latter would be frightened by the flames, and she was not young. I did not wait to see them drive off, though I kissed each little boy, sleepy and still unafraid as they were, though Alicky wanted to know where they were going. "To see a friend," I said. I pulled my bed-gown to me, began to run as soon as they were out of sight, and did not stop till, sobbing for breath, I saw the leaping flames close and felt them scorch me. There was one way, only one, to save something of Andrew's years of work, for he would be fighting the fire by now and would not think of it. I must try to save the seed, the single eye of Polyphemus, the almost mature and precious gourd which hung from the queen tree in the centre of the planting. There was only one way I could probably take, surveying the wall of flame on the house side blown by the wind. That was the avenue down which I had stumbled, it seemed a lifetime ago, to give birth to the children. It was possible that the fire had not yet reached that part: at any rate, I must try.

## Thirty-one

I found the place, having hurried past the open space between the house and the forest where I could see the black active shapes of Andrew and the farm-men clear against the flames. They had been handing a chain of water-buckets from the well, as the stream was low, and flinging the contents on the fire; but the high wind made this useless and the flames still swirled despite them. Now I saw them start to dig a trench to try to stop the fire from spreading towards the house. The wind veered this way and that. I did not let them see me pass by as I was afraid that they would feel obliged to prevent me and waste their time from what they were at. I was glad the children had gone.

The ruins of bracken and bramble at my entry-place were lit brightly and had begun to shrivel with the heat. The fire was not far off and looked soon to engulf the whole forest. I held my gown about me and begun to run, battling to defeat the flames and the contrary wind. Down the long corridor, lit as though by a thousand candles, I went; the hut at the end was a dark square shape, its roof already beginning to smoulder. There would barely be time to reach, by whatever means, the high place where the seed-box hung. I knew as I ran that I must find something to stand on; perhaps I could pile some logs, or shake the tree.

I was angry as well as afraid. Eight years of Andrew's work and life wasted, because a devil with a tinder had come here in the night, and had made the trees blaze up like dry paper. A tinder, because of me; because of Clun's thwarted lust, his being whipped like a malefactor. Was he to go free for this?

Then I came on him and saw that he would never again be free. He was lying between one trunk and the next, with a knife in his back, and he was dead. I knew the knife was Saginaw's.

I did not wait; there was nothing I could do for Clun. Now I could see the queen tree, her bronzed foliage shining in the firelight, her great fecund breadth and height soraring into the orange darkness. There was no foothold, no hand-hold here: she had been too well pruned. I looked up into the upper branches and searched frantically for the seed, remembering how I had once held in my hand its ancestor, the time Andrew showed it me when I was young. I remembered the big curved shape and the shine like chestnut fruit, and I would know it again. But it was not there. Had Clun taken it? But he would not have known of the queen tree and the seed. Besides Andrew himself, there was only one other who knew.

It was then I saw the Indian, his face smeared with soot, naked except for his leather breeches. He carried something between his hands and I knew it was the seed-case. I cried out and he turned and looked at me. I saw then that the tears were running down his cheeks, making runnels in the soot.

"Where are you going?" I said. It was one of the few times I had ever spoken to him. "Give me the seed. The men out there need your help with the digging. There are not enough of them."

"No luck for white man. It will all burn."

"So you are leaving?" I knew it was useless to cajole him;

his jet-black eyes looked at me with a glint of defiance, the first emotion I had ever seen in them. He nodded. I said again "Give me the seed. It is Andrew's. I will take it to him."

"Tree belong to no white man. It is my people's, the Erie people. It will not grow again for Andrew."

"Saginaw, you have killed a man and a woman. If they know they will hang you. I will tell them nothing, if you give me the seed." I knew that Clun's body would be consumed; if the knife were drawn out of him it would be thought he had perished in the fire. The Indian had not moved again; all about us was roaring swaying flame, but he was still.

"I kill man. He make fire. But I kill no woman." He sounded puzzled and I faced him.

"You killed Penuel. She would not bear your child and she died of it after you said you were done with her. Give me the seed and I will say nothing of that, or the man." I knew, God knows, that he would not hang for Penuel. But I hoped to frighten him about Clun.

He came towards me slowly. "You and Andrew are blood-brothers," I said; I had to shout because of the roaring of the fire. It was unbearably hot; soon my clothes and hair would start to smoulder, and I did not know how he endured the heat any more than I. "You promised to work together till the trees were grown."

"I have worked. They grew. Now they are dead. They will not live again for him. This place has no luck. I am going away."

I said desperately "You have worked hard with the trees, as hard as Andrew himself. But the seed is not yours. It was given to my husband by the chief of the tribe, for trying to save his son." If I could only lure the Indian from this place, get him nearer Andrew who would make him give up what he held, even in the midst of wrestling with the flames, the lack of water, the stray cruel wind!

Saginaw had ceased weeping and stood looking at me so that his eyes focussed beyond me; I might have been a pillar of stone. He said "The seed is the gift of my tribe. They know of fire, for fire and sword passed over their land till it was a desert. They bore the seed with them when they went. I will take it back to the father of my tribe where he lives across the great water."

I saw the flames light up the interior of the hut and the birch and bracken bed where Penuel had lain, where I myself had lain briefly at the birth. I screamed "You swore to my husband that you would aid him. Now you take away the seed without a word. You are no friend to him. Did the other man, who started the fire, give you silver to leave him in peace? You should have guarded the forest. The fire is your fault." I hardly knew what I was saying, for soon now neither of us could get away; a circle of fire was about us and I saw the near undergrowth take on a running low flame which sparked and spread across our way of escape. "You took his silver, and then you killed him," I said. Only a taunt now could make him listen.

"It is not true that I took silver. I killed him when he made fire here. Soon we will both of us burn." He sounded now as if there were no escape, that he was resigned to stay and die here. I said, holding out my hands, "Give me the seed. I will take it through the fire to my husband." My words sounded childish, yet even with my skin beginning to scorch and my hair and clothes smouldering, I was certain that if he would give me the seed-box I could win through somehow and protect it; the fire might burn my body, but I would save the seed.

Then there came a great crashing of timber; the trees were falling. I saw the Indian's eyes widen so that their whites showed; suddenly he moved forward and caught me to him, thrusting my face against his shoulder and taking my weight. I tried to cry out and could not, stifled by the heat and the rancid smell of his flesh; but if I were to turn my head away there was the fire, all about us now. Saginaw was running; running through the crackling undergrowth that must burn his feet, running towards the last patch of clear night sky. I felt my clothes and arms burn; we were both of us on fire; we were within it, moving too swiftly to be consumed, but the searing pain made me gasp, and my hair was ablaze. Witches and saints through the ages had felt this agony as their end, and so did I; and in the midst of it tried to think of my love for Andrew and its late, full and perfect consummation; I could take the memory with me wherever my spirit should go, and forget the scorching agonising present. Suddenly I felt a mighty wind within the fire: Saginaw screamed, thrust something between my breasts and flung me out and beyond the falling tree. I can remember crawling, with the warm seed pressed against me, out to where the moss was almost cool. My smouldering head tortured me and I beat at it with all my strength to put out the flames. Then I fell down between the road and the wall, and knew no more.

When I awoke it was to pain, and the sound of a man's sobbing. I could not see, for something covered my eyes; they felt sticky, and hurt me. I tried to grope through the darkness to where Andrew was, but I could feel nothing clearly; my hands must be bandaged, and my body. I tried to turn towards him and it was such torture that I cried aloud. I heard him call my name.

"Primrose. Primrose. You are safe now. You should not have done it—for me—"

"Is the seed safe?"

"Safe, my darling. Do not speak of it any more. You must rest; try to sleep."

"What hour is it? I cannot see if 'tis night or day."

"You will—when they take off the bandages, please God— ah, Primrose, to have done that for me—you should never have gone there—forgive me, and grow better, with time it will heal—"

"Where is Saginaw? He saved me, I think."

"He is dead. We found him beneath the remains of the tree, and that other—"

I tried to sit up. "Andrew, you must take away the knife—it must never be known, they must think he burned, otherwise they may blame you—because of me—"

"They know it was Saginaw. Thornton has been here, and Augusta. They send their love and say that when you are better, they will call again. Rest now, darling."

"Am I badly burned?" It seemed a foolish question, I knew, but if I were a twisted ruined thing whom Andrew could no longer love, or if I were blind, or had to wear a wig, any such thing, it was better to die now, before he saw what I had become. At least my mind was clear. No tears would run from under my gummed eyelids, underneath the bandages. I must have lost hair, eyelashes, perhaps beauty. I remembered my mother's sad life with her ruined face. Must I become such a one? I prayed then that I might not be like that; not for my own sake, but my husband's.

He was still sobbing. I felt myself smile, and thought; at least my mouth is not scarred. We must wait, and see. I must try to comfort Andrew; this was strange, when so many times it was he who had comforted me. "You have not lost everything," I said. "There are still the beaver-skins." I was tired; strange that talk should tire one so soon. "I can sleep now," I told him.

"If I had lost you—nothing else matters—thank God we found you when we did, for I had given up all hope—"

"The children matter," I said drowsily. "Are they still at the Admiral's?"

"We are all at the Admiral's, my darling. Pless burned."

"Pless." At one time it would have seemed of importance. Now it meant nothing to me at all. If Thornton wanted his heritage, he could claim it. Perhaps, by now, he did not.

## Thirty two

I GREW BETTER. When the physician came to remove the bandages from my eyes I had Andrew by me, holding both my hands. We both knew I might have been blinded, or at the least that I might not see as well as I had done. In fact my sight was at the first something imperfect, but the doctor said he had known of cases where time improved the matter, and certainly it has done so in mine. Being protected against the Indian's body had saved my features, and my hair and lashes would grow again, though at first I was bald as a scarecrow, and wept at the sight of myself in a mirror. There was a scar on my temple, which would whiten with time, and other scars on my hands and feet and my back.

The Admiral came to visit me, stumping in with his silver-topped cane soon after the bandages had been taken off. "Ye are a brave woman, to be sure, ma'am! Never thought I'd meet a heroine! Most of 'em are fools, but ye have revised my opinion of the sex, to be sure ye have!" Then he took my hand with an odd tenderness. "This is a scarred little hand," he said, "but never fear, it will thread a needle again," and he kissed it. Andrew and I had a great affection for him, and he for us, by the time we left his house, where he had kindly accommodated us. Thornton and Augusta were anxious for us to come to them, but it was not thought wise that I should travel yet, and Augusta was expecting her baby.

Yes, I had much to be thankful for. But being of a shallow nature I often grieved, for Andrew's sake, that my body was no longer perfect, for he had loved it. My breasts were saved, and the front of me; and the rest could be pressed down against the pillows, but it took a long time for me to believe that he could truly love me again as he had done.

He knew my thoughts though I said nothing of them. One day he came to me saying "Primrose, if I were to lose an eye or an arm would you cease to love me?"

"No, surely not; you would be the same man."

"Then when my hair is grey as it soon may be, will I seem a different being to you?"

I set my head to one side, trying to fathom his meaning. "You do not trust me, you see," he said. "You believe, do you not, that my love for you is but an admiration of outward features?"

"I am a woman. We have little except appearance to commend us."

"That is a mistaken saying. If it were true there would be no devoted old couples in the world, yet I know of those who have been wed for forty years and take no heed of wrinkles or white hair, or the loss of teeth."

He took my hand. "Cannot you understand that although I loved you dearly, I love you now even more when you have risked your life for my whim? No matter how badly scarred you were, if it had been on your pretty face, if your hair might never grow again, if no matter how many disasters had befallen your looks, do you not know I would love you still? Looks signify little; what matters is that you should not grow bitter. Think how much worse it could have been, and then forget it for the most part. I love you and you are my wife. Do you still love me, your husband?"

"I had never thought to hear you make so long a speech," I said, and cast my arms about his neck. Then he told me we were going to live in Canada. "Thornton made it clear that there was no urgency over the matter of Pless; all the same—" Andrew smiled—"before the fire, he had ridden down into Yorkshire to see Beatrice Elmay for himself, and examine the records at the parish church of Thursby. It is a different matter now the estate is worth nothing except the value of a few charred stumps."

"Then Clun had told him of the marriage?" I blushed deeply. Had I given myself to Clun that night, how would I feel now?

"Clun could keep his tongue still about very little. He is not greatly mourned." But, as I heard later, Andrew had had to answer questions about the death of Clun, and it was by God's mercy that the servants were able to give evidence that he had spent all of that day with me. So our loving had not destroyed him, but rather saved him. "It is time, I think," Andrew said now, "that we should pack our bags with such gear as we have left, and take the children aboard a ship to where I can be a furrier and trapper as well as an owner at auctions. There is profit in the business, and it is a good country for the boys to grow up in. There are no decadents there, like Clun; if they come out, they do not long endure it."

"I will come gladly," I told him. He looked at me narrowly, and I saw relief in his face.

"How thankful I am!" he said. "I was afraid that going overseas would not be to your liking."

"Then you would have stayed, no doubt."

"Maybe I would."

"And plant your trees again? Never fear, Andrew, I do but tease. What is there to part with, except sad memories?" I turned to look at him. "I never think now of Pless," I said, "but to you, it meant your forest. Do you still grieve for that?"

"And the Admiralty contract? Not now. When first I saw the flames leap, I was like a child whose favourite toy has been taken. Then I set myself to fight the fire, and then I found you lying where you were, and knew that nothing mattered but that you were safe. The trees have been; I have grown them; it has been done."

"And you have the seed," I exclaimed. He laughed.

"Our sons may try to grow the seed if they desire; I am too old. There is land enough in Canada, but they may have trouble with the Indian tribes if news spreads. Driven to the barren north-west as they were, the Erie people had not such soil as had once lain about their lake. Some day I shall ride to visit the tribe again, and tell them of the seed and of Saginaw."

He looked down at his hands for moments and I realised that he and the Indian had not met with one another after I had told Andrew of Penuel and her death. I resolved to say nothing, for what was the good of surmising what would have happened? Instead I smiled and said "Then you will be away from me half the year. I had best resign myself to being left alone in a wood cabin, with a shot-gun; there will be no keeping you from your travels."

"I will always return," he said.

And so it proved. For the first two years Andrew's fur-trading occupied him so greatly on the business side, which despite his labours had been somewhat neglected while the trees grew, that he was away from home seldom. Later he began to go on his trapping-journeys again, and down to Montreal to sell the furs. I did not try to detain him, for women who try to put leading-reins on their man have only themselves to blame if he becomes idle and spiritless, or pursues other women. Our house was made of black stone, and Andrew built it with his own hands; he said he would not trust to a timber place lest it go on fire. Behind us are great slopes of mountain and forest, and a

lake where the boys swim. I am glad the forest is no nearer;
I shall never again be free of foreboding when among trees.
The boys know the story of the Polyphemus seed and have
sworn one day to plant it, though I doubt if Alicky has the
steady application his father had, and Jamie will more likely
turn out a scholar, like his father's father, though he looks like
me.

I have borne five other children. Two of them are girls,
Penuel and Marjory. They would be in danger of becoming
spoilt by their father if it were not for having so many brothers.
With such constant bearing I have somewhat lost my figure,
and Miss Jule's cookery lessons have never been more necessary.
The girls help me, and have been taught to sew; we are making,
the three of us, a patchwork quilt, as I promised myself I would
do long ago. Also, we have some interest in botany, and there
are many plants here the same as at home, as well as many
different. Andrew and the boys tend a flower-garden beside
the house, which is a thing not often met with owing to the
short Canadian summer.

We are happy. This is a country where every practical
skill is needed if one is to live, and everyone met with is a
friend, for they may have travelled from hundreds of miles
away. Trappers come down from the north parts with
marvellous furs for Andrew; wolf, fox, lynx, beaver. I have a
wolfskin hood, to protect my face from the cold, and sometimes
when we ride out by sleigh I tuck a fur rug about myself and
the children, but that is all I take to do with it; truth to tell I am
sorry for the poor animals which must be trapped and killed.
But it makes our living, and Andrew works hard, as he has
done all his life. His hair is grey now, as he foretold. Often as I
look at him I feel a softness come into my thoughts, and when I
catch his blue gaze it is returned to me in like kind: yes, we
love each other. It took many years, and many a mile by sea
and land, to bring me to my present state of contentment, but
I am happy now; happier than when, on that day long ago,

I climbed the branch of Pless tree to find crab-apples and let them hit a stranger in the garden, who was looking at a handful of earth.